D1809814

Praise for books by Matt Howard

'A charming experience. There are times when Howard's humour bites deep' *Sydney Morning Herald*

'Howard has a deft, wry, comic touch and a great sense of the stultifying atmosphere to which anyone who has grown up in Australia's outer suburbs will relate' *Sun-Herald*

'Howard is unafraid of sentiment' *Bulletin*

'Gently comic, surprisingly tender' *Adelaide Advertiser*

'In his debut novel, *Street Furniture*, Matt Howard displayed a certain droll, youthful touch that endeared him to readers and critics alike. *Taking Off* sees him continuing in the same vein ... to clever effect' *Australian Book Review*

Matt Howard's first novel *Street Furniture* (2004) was set in Sydney, garnered some great reviews, and has been optioned to a group of Californian film-makers. Matt's second novel *Taking Off* (2008) is about the ups and downs of travel. Matt keeps changing his mind so lives in Sydney, then Melbourne, then Sydney. Currently in Sydney he is eyeing Melbourne.

a novel

Ethan Grout

Matt Howard

PIER  9

Published in 2010 by Pier 9, an imprint of Murdoch Books Pty Limited

Murdoch Books Australia
Pier 8/9
23 Hickson Road
Millers Point NSW 2000
Phone: +61 (0) 2 8220 2000
Fax: +61 (0) 2 8220 2558
www.murdochbooks.com.au

Murdoch Books UK Limited
Erico House, 6th Floor
93–99 Upper Richmond Road
Putney, London SW15 2TG
Phone: +44 (0) 20 8785 5995
Fax: +44 (0) 20 8785 5985
www.murdochbooks.co.uk

Publisher: Colette Vella
Editor: Julia Stiles
Project Editor: Kate Fitzgerald
Designer: Design by Committee

Text copyright © Matt Howard 2010
The moral right of the author has been asserted.
Design copyright © Murdoch Books Pty Limited 2010
Cover photography by iStock and Stock.XCHNG
Author photograph by Jenny Unnegard

The events and characters depicted in this book are entirely fictional and are not intended to portray actual events.

All rights reserved. No part of this publication may be reproduced, stored in a retrieval system or transmitted in any form or by any means, electronic, mechanical, photocopying, recording or otherwise, without the prior written permission of the publisher.

National Library of Australia Cataloguing-in-Publication Data

Author: Howard, Matt
Title: Ethan Grout / Matt Howard.
ISBN: 978-1-74196-898-9 (pbk.)
Dewey Number: A823.4

PRINTED IN AUSTRALIA

FSC
Mixed Sources
Product group from well-managed
forests and other controlled sources

Cert no. SGS-COC-005088
www.fsc.org
© 1996 Forest Stewardship Council

The paper this book is printed on is certified by the © 1996 Forest Stewardship Council A.C. (FSC). Griffin Press holds FSC chain of custody SGS-COC-005088. FSC promotes environmentally responsible, socially beneficial and economically viable management of the world's forests.

For

Simon Proud
Kate Farrar
Matt Wakeham
Ana Kingi
Maya Donevska
Cheryl Akle
Magnus Fuxner
Karin Veghed
Erick Lundqvist

1. Small Quarters

'So what do you do?'

'Nothing.'

Her face is expectant. She wants more. Like me.

'I left my job last week when Dad, you know, declined.'

'So you'll go back?'

'No, I had a farewell cake and everything.'

Who talks about cake at a funeral?

'It was Dad's idea to quit. My job I mean,' I explain, giving the decision some merit.

She's waiting on me to scramble into the empty back seat of the sleek black sedan. I could live in that amount of space. I pretty much do.

'He thought I'd been in the one place way too long. Well he would, wouldn't he.' It isn't a question and she doesn't answer.

'Ethan, you take care.' The lady says it kindly and I smile thanks as she rejoins her friends, my father's friends, as they reminisce alongside their less sombre cars. From what I know Dad pretty much met all these people while working – changing jobs and locations every few months, collecting friends as he went. This woman had partied at our place years back, when a bunch of them no doubt found themselves in the same city at the same time. I used to love watching them arrive, knowing that the house would be complete with noise and life for hours and I'd happily fall asleep to its rhythms.

A couple of other faces in my father's gang look vaguely familiar and I scan the numberplates. Three matches.

I realise by the driver's stiff pose that he is waiting for his car to fill with more family; I leave it a beat before disappointing him.

'It's just me today,' I tell the back of his head.

The 'today' is *so* superfluous.

'Okey doke,' he replies.

So much for the stiff demeanour.

I can't exactly have the driver drop me at Baxter's so I start to say, 'Take me back to the house', then realise I'm crying. I look out the window, allowing the lowering sun to warm my face and decide it must be around four. Possibly as late as five past.

'Okey doke.'

■ ■ ■

'So, Ethan – what score do you give me?'

'Score?' I ask, knowing this time it doesn't relate to a film.

'Out of ten … Markus Grout … in the role of Ethan's dad.'

The nurse leaves us alone. She told me earlier that he was going to be lucid right till the end and, true to form, he's been chatting up a storm all afternoon.

'Nine,' I say.

'What did I lose a mark for?'

'That's a damn fine rating – be content.'

'We talked about using *that* word around me, even to yourself,' Dad chides me on the 'c' word.

'Hey, don't forget I flipped off my job just yesterday,' Ethan the fresh new radical reminds him, and he smiles. Most parents yearn for a sensible child – not Markus.

'So …?'

'Okay – the lost mark is due to the story ending too soon,' I say, trying to keep it light, which he manages to do so effortlessly, but me – I get all unstuck.

He wants to be marked short for leaving me alone so often as a kid, when the only thing that sucks now is him leaving me alone for good.

'Ethan … live it, buddy – live *your* life.'

■ ■ ■

That's what he told me as I cried and his hand stilled in mine. They weren't his last words but they were his most lucid. And now that the only person to whom I am important has gone, and I've finally realised he isn't going to be replaced by any of the folk I drifted with at Auto World for years, it is down to me.

Live your fucking life.

■ ■ ■

Now I'm standing outside Dad's place, my old place – Sleepy Hollow – considering if I should go inside. But like this morning, as I waited for the black car, I don't. Neither of us has lived here for ages, in fact I'm not sure now if my father ever really did. Inside it's probably empty.

The porch light is on, though it's still day, quarter past four I reckon. Ironically Dad left it on to ward against break-ins, but nothing screams *no one is home* quite like a lightbulb competing with sunshine.

The bungalow is not so big but way too large for one person. I lived here from the time my memory kicked in to well after school, but the house looks like any other to me. In fact, I still pick it out by the rusting numbers on the letterbox.

'Ethan? Is that you?'

Over the side fence a couple of eyes were looking at me.

'Yeah, hi Mr Lopez.'

'You remember me? It must be forever since you lived here.'

'Only six years.'

'Is that all?' Mr Lopez muses. 'Seems you were never really living here at all.'

He probably means my father, but it's true of me too, I guess.

Mr Lopez's eyes move along the line of battered grey palings, which gradually descend in height, allowing him to ascend in height just as smoothly.

'You look smart.'

'It was Dad's funeral today.'

Mr Lopez's face flushes but I wave off his embarrassment.

'It was only a matter of time,' I say, acknowledging the inevitability that surrounded his death.

'I wish I'd known. We would have come to offer our respects.' Mr Lopez steps over what remains of the fence and joins me in front of my old place, inspecting it as you would a prospective home purchase. Arms folded, critical eye.

'How was he? In the end I mean?'

'Good,' I say automatically. 'I mean, you know, in good spirits. In fact, he got married just a month back.'

'Married! He certainly never let the grass grow beneath his feet!' With those words, Mr Lopez is reddening again.

'I was the one mowing it,' I joke, so as to remove the awkwardness, but I end up sounding bitter instead.

Mr Lopez eyes the lawn, now kept in shape by a local guy my dad found when I moved out.

'Markus was certainly a busy man. I rarely saw him here, even after you were gone ...' Mr Lopez is quick enough to stop himself from observing that he hadn't seen much of my dad before I left either.

I remember how I'd leave the lights on around the house, just like the one on the porch now, to try to convince the neighbours, and anyone else who'd worry about a kid who lived on his own, that I wasn't the only one in the place. It wasn't squatters I feared – the company would have been nice.

'Nice to see you, Mr Lopez – say hi to Mrs Lopez for me.' I offer my hand and leave him in the front yard. It's been good to see a familiar face, even if it has sagged a bit, but now more than ever I've nowhere to be and I'm keen to get there.

■ ■ ■

The tram shudders along Swanston Street and I try not to calculate the variance between the number of people getting on and off at each stop. Ahead I can see the Baxter building – the pub part looks to be quite busy. Dusk will have conceded to night by the time I get upstairs, and I make out, from my seat on the tram, the light coming from my room.

There is a separate residents' entrance, which means I don't need to go through the crowd downstairs, but I decide, as I mostly always do, to wade through the main bar. It's even busier than a regular Friday and it feels nice to come home to a place with so much life in it. No wonder Dad liked the place back in the day. Most everyone at Auto World was mystified why I would choose to live here however – being as it's never dark, never empty, and always noisy. Noisy enough to induce slumber. They didn't know me.

I circle around the huddles of suits, cliques of Friday casuals, and the larger groups of regulars. And then I see them.

Between me and the internal staircase that leads up to the poky rooms are faces from earlier today. Busy waking my dad.

I could turn on my heels, head back to the street and scurry up to my bedsit from out the front, but that really would be pathetic. They can't see me, my father's gang; I reckon they can't see much in fact. I find a stool that allows me not to look entirely stranded and enables me to listen to their reminiscences without being spotted.

Seems most of them worked with him at various times. Some were cinematographers like him; some were in lighting, others sound, and a garishly painted woman was in makeup and hair. The lady who asked after my job was, as I recall, a film editor. She worked with my father on many movies over the years and more than once she and some of his other colleagues collected at our house after a shoot and I'd listen in on their stories as I'm doing now.

'What about the time, on that shoot in New Zealand, Markus managed to miss shooting that car blowing up after they'd spent the best part of the week setting up the explosion.'

'Well, I don't think he slept the entire time we were there, so they were lucky he shot anything much at all!'

The anecdotes ricochet around the gang and I move my stool a little closer. And just like with Mr Lopez earlier I hear, 'Ethan? Is that you?'

I smile and the editor waves me over.

'Did you come to join in the wake?' she asks, a little surprised that I'd stalked them.

'Not really. This is my home.'

They all look stunned, though I'm sure several of them virtually live in bars, judging by the fine colour of their noses.

'Upstairs,' I offer by way of explanation.

'Would you like a drink?' the editor asks.

'Thanks, but I've got to get going actually,' I lie.

'I guess a young fellow like you would prefer to spend tonight with his mates,' she laughs, winking.

I nod as I don't want to lie again. I don't move though.

'We're just remembering some of the funny times, working with your dad,' the editor says.

This time I get up to head for the front door. They all raise their glasses and the editor offers me a card.

'Give me a call, Ethan – if you find it hard to get a new job. We can always use people – extras, gophers.'

I could pass as an extra, I reckon.

'It's not glamorous, mind,' she adds.

A few of her mates laugh knowingly.

'Yes. I work on a soap opera. I admit it,' she confides with a smile. 'Bigger things in the pipeline though.'

'Cheers,' I say.

Without reading the card I pull out my wallet and slip it inside and see the gift card I received from my work colleagues: my reward for close on a decade.

I set to leave again and the editor touches my hand.

'Your friends will help you move on, Ethan.'

I'll try not to dwell on that.

■ ■ ■

It may seem weird to most anyone that I'd go to a mall on the night of my father's funeral. And it is.

The gift card is for Books Etcetera and I plan to make for their etcetera section. But first I head to the checkout to discover how much value is on the card. A young guy with Tintin hair tries to get my card to give it up but he seems to be struggling.

'We just got a new computer system and this card is the old type.'

'I only got it like a week ago.'

'Yes, anything before yesterday is old.'

'So how do I work out how much I have to spend?'

'I can only get a remaining balance once you buy something. They didn't tell you what it's worth?'

'No, it's a gift, a surprise.'

'Do you have an idea how much it might be for?'

'I haven't really thought about it. I guess $100 or something like that. Maybe $150 if they were feeling generous.'

Tintin makes a thinking face, with a finger pointing out his chin. 'What you can do is select what you want and then I can swipe your purchases and the card. It will let me know if you've spent too much or what change is due.'

'Okay. Thanks.'

I find the DVD section and work out my strategy. I've got plenty of time so I decide to make my way from A to Z. Working on the dream scenario of $200 I calculate my armful and recalculate each time I add to my selection.

There are so many great films – some I've been meaning to see since they were first advertised on the massive billboard outside my window.

By the time I've hit the T's I need to reprioritise the lot and ditch the weakest each time I want to add one. It's dark outside so I've no idea what time it is, but there are definitely more people leaving the store now than coming in. Tintin's colleagues are looking suspiciously like they plan to haul the shutters down at any moment.

I rush through the last few shelves and carry my stack to the counter. Tintin swipes through the pile of DVDs – mostly he gives approving nods and even a 'Yes' to one. This is surprisingly reassuring given he is a complete stranger to me.

'Now, the card.'

I look expectantly, deciding which ones left behind might quickly be resurrected to the 'in crowd' if money allows.

'Uh, seems you've gone over.'

'How much?'

'Uh, *a lot.*'

'Give me a clue here,' I say, stretching my neck to see what the display says – probably *Loser*.

'Dude, you have twenty-five dollars.'

'I'm over by twenty-five dollars?'

'No, you have, in total, twenty-five to spend.'

And there's the spoiler alert.

'Oh. Just this one then I guess.' I point out the fresh copy of *The Fantastic Four* and he says he'd bag it for me except that would take it over my limit.

'Have a nice night!' Tintin says brightly as I slope off.

Outside it has started to rain, at an intermittent wiper rate, and I wait at the tram stop. Me and *The Fantastic Four*.

■ ■ ■

The residents' entrance opens right onto a laneway near its intersection with Swanston Street. I'm not sure if my father's friends are still downstairs but I'll leave it a mystery I think. The stairwell looks a perfect place to pass out drunk or even overdose, but fortunately there is no need to step over anyone tonight. The dimly lit hallway has a few slashes of light at foot level and one is mine.

I lock the door behind me and the noise from the revellers downstairs is now drowned out by the street buzz rising up from Swanston. My single open window catches the shouts and laughter and hurls them in at me. But it's better than silence. Underneath the window is a huge fish tank – the size and shape of a bar fridge that has toppled over. Mister Fantastic is alone now and he's a little dwarfed by his surroundings.

The room is big enough to fit my double bed but little else besides. I strip off my soon-to-be job-seeking suit and turn off the light, which immediately brightens the outside. As I get into bed I look out the window and there he is. Plastered across the billboard that is my view of the world, freshly rolled out since this morning, surrounded by a frame of flickering lightbulbs, and replacing the Advanced Medical Solutions ad about making *it* last longer. The virtual stranger who, pretty soon it seems, will be the only family I'll have left.

2. Listing

The street wakes me even before the birds have realised they're on duty. I wait until daylight joins in the sequence of wakeup calls before opening my eyes. Mister Fantastic is still alive and not listing like the others took it in turn to do. The black suit hanging over the clothes rack reminds me that I have more to do today than eat. I need to start the whole job search thing at the internet café. In total I reckon I'll likely get through the whole day with a maximum of ten words spoken – and all those to bored cashiers.

It seemed futile to sell Dad's house to enable me not to work just so I could … what?

Though I have less numbers in my mobile than fingers to prod at it with, and its use as timekeeper is limited, I always leave it on anyway, and every week or so it'll need charging. The beeping gets me out of bed; I find it under the jeans I last wore three days ago, and hook it up. The sun is at half past eight, just askew of the clocktower above the town hall down the street. That clock stopped four years back and time has stood still since.

It's hard to ignore the giant billboard at any time, even when the frame of lights is dimmed, but now that my recently acquired stepbrother is beaming across at me from it, hip in Diesel, it's impossible. Travis's mother was at the wedding of course, at my father's bedside, and finally at the funeral. Her name's Joy and she's lasted longer than Dad. They met when both were in the hospital, married as if they were on a bender in Vegas – with more bald heads celebrating than at an Olympic swim meet – and almost immediately my father went one way and she the other. Like he and my own mother had done decades back.

Joy wore a black bandana yesterday and Travis a suit that probably came gratis with a modeling gig. Both looked beautiful in their own way – though you expect that more at a wedding than a funeral. They, however, wore the humble expression of interlopers and scurried off before I could suggest they accompany me in the empty car.

The weather is awesome for winter. Zero chance of rain. Even if I used my television for much more than DVDs I'd avoid the weather forecasts – I prefer to push my head out the window each morning. There has to be some element of surprise.

And my final check – the sell sheet from today's newspaper. Outside the newsagent across the road and slightly to the left, beneath Travis's white smile, today's breaking news, held together by a lattice rack of rusted wire – *MADONNA DUMPS AUSSIE NANNY*. A slow news day as well.

■ ■ ■

The tram that goes by the hospital is virtually empty so I take a seat being slowly heated by the early sunshine. I'd have walked but today feels a bit lonely. A guy, wearing a T-shirt even I'd have relegated to the classification of *indoors only*, gets on the tram at one point, wrestles with a window, gets it open and then promptly gets off. Out of the city centre the tram driver takes his foot off the brake and I consider if I might do the same.

Weaving through the smokers outside the hospital entrance, their hacking and conversations drowned out by the fuss created by a helicopter dropping onto the roof, I trek the familiar route to the cafeteria on the mezzanine level.

The fact that I've no one to visit now means I'm the only one here with nothing to lose.

'Hi buddy, what would you like today?'

He recognises me. Please don't ask after my dad.

'Chicken and rice please.'

'Here you go,' he says when he's done placing a generous pile of chicken on a substantial stack of rice. 'You certainly like chicken, don't you?'

'Thanks.'

Five words to go.

I slide my tray onto a table and almost immediately a tired-looking woman, with a clutch of lanyards hanging from her neck, plunks herself down at the next table. I smile at her lonely soul and she smiles back. No one is looking at me – contemplating the guy eating by himself – I'm the same as everyone else. Within seconds the woman is joined by a friend and they set about talking about this and that and I'm again the odd one out.

The tram back to the city is fuller this time and I hop off before it starts its struggle down Swanston Street and head for an internet café. I have to create an all-purpose résumé – one that can be attached to any application and not look too specific. I spend two words on the cashier and take my designated computer.

After an hour or so I realise that one résumé is not going to be applicable to all the jobs on Seek that look like possibilities. Each time I find a position in retail or sales or hospitality or any other crap, in fact any field that's not bothered by degrees, the requirements are still so specific that the résumé has to be tweaked again and again. The thing I have going for me, I'd imagined, was over nine years at one place, but I'm guessing that may be the exact same thing that'll work against me.

My last job was office gold – print stations, coffee fund and farewell cards. There was a large staff, which was entirely necessary as Auto World was very serious about overcomplicating things. Each time I apply for something that sounds exactly the same I get nauseous and apply for something completely left field, and then back again. Hours pass and I've lost track of what I've applied for and which version of my résumé I've sent to whom.

My cover note also changes in response to the role – sometimes I'm creative, sometimes I'm fastidious, and sometimes I'm even a leader.

Like I told the editor lady at Dad's funeral yesterday, he was the one who encouraged me to finally quit the job I'd had since leaving school. You'd have thought that after so long I'd have made as many friends and memories as my father, who was always as entouraged as a cashed-up hip-hop star. He told me that had all come about by mixing it up and that's what he wanted me to do.

'Life happens in episodes,' he told me, the film guy in him coming to the fore. 'Maybe you just need to speed up those episodes, Ethan.'

As I considered his opinion and prevaricated through his final weeks, the ritualistic returning to work of a forgotten colleague with baby in tow had me surprising the fuck out of my boss for once. The escapee gathered a crowd around her stroller in the lunchroom and not just once proclaimed how amazed she was that nothing about the place and none of us had changed one bit in eighteen months. My fellow inmates all took this as a great compliment. That topped it off nicely.

My dad was pleased no end and I let him think it was all down to his sage advice. He told me not to worry about money – I could sell or rent out our old house if need be. But I wasn't worried about money.

He went so far as to assure me that he and Joy had agreed not to alter their wills when they got married: he'd look after me and she Travis; just the thought of it caught me off guard until it was trumped by him referring to Joy as 'your new mother'. I actually laughed and Dad followed me into happy tears. He was not without his sense of humour – I mean he had shot that Bollywood suckjob *Jimesh Finds Love*.

Somehow I've been able to continue emailing applications whilst musing about my last job and Dad's final scenes. Who knows what I've sent out. I decide to check the email address I've been quoting and already I've had three automatically generated rejections. About ten per cent. Still room for a lot more disappointment.

There's no need for words as I pay for these past four hours and I'm back on Swanston Street. The lack of communication suddenly hits me and I'd happily blow my word quota on a lost tourist, but none approach me.

Halfway down the lane that intersects with Swanston to create a corner for Baxter's is the place I mostly get dinner from – if it's not the occasional Maccas or the even more often *nothing*. The Good Luck Restaurant is my most commonly dialled number. By a long shot. It's preferable to call so I don't have to sit waiting for number 52 to slide about the wok, while the beautiful lilac light in the bug zapper commits nightly carnage. The sun is not yet finished with the day and shafts of light beam through the unattached buildings on the far side of the lane, meaning the insects are not yet as hungry as I am. So I decide to request my number live.

I make like I'm reading the menu board and after a respectable time I approach the familiar face.

'Fifty-two thanks.'

I'm not sure if that counts as two words or three – best to err on the side of caution – my quota is all used up. No more words today. Shouldn't be a stretch – I'm almost home.

'Of course,' Zhen says, turning around, and announcing with all the lethargy he can muster, 'Fifty-two' at the folk through the servery.

I watch through the hole in the wall that showcases the working kitchen as Zhen's family go about their business. None of them look like they'll end up on *Masterchef* but they are all part of something – something bigger than one.

To compensate for not being in a position to say thanks while collecting together the plastic handles of the carry bag, I offer a massive smile to Zhen, who shows me his teeth in return.

The bar is quite empty save for barnacle people – the regulars. I nod at a few of them and leap two stairs at a time with my bag of Good Luck feeling warm as it bangs against my leg. As I'm seeking out my key I can hear a noise I've definitely heard before. Opening the door, the noise gets louder. My phone!

Dropping the food on top of my bed I collect the phone off of the floor and disconnect the charger. The screen says, *Dad.*

'Hello?'

'Hello, Ethan? This is Joy.'

'Oh, um, hi, I thought it was um ...'

'Ethan – I'm so sorry – I shouldn't have used your dad's phone. It's just that I wanted to call you and I didn't know your number. I should have transferred it to mine.'

'That's okay – it was nice for a second.'

'I feel terrible.'

'It's fine, honestly.'

'Thanks. How are you going?'

'Not too bad. What about *you*?'

I feel bad for stressing the *you* as if I'm expecting her to keel over now that Dad has established the precedent.

'I'm doing okay. I miss Markus. Your dad. Is that weird? I realise I barely know him really. Knew him.'

'You made him happy – nothing weird about that.'

'Thanks, Ethan. I wanted to excuse me and Travis for not really catching up with you yesterday – I didn't want to get in the way.'

'No problem.'

'Also, I wondered if you would like to come over for dinner this week. Maybe Tuesday if that suits you. Travis will be here – he's in training for fashion week. We can laugh at him together.'

I laugh with her now – she's mocking her model son to me, the steppiest of stepbrothers.

'Sure, okay. Thanks,' I say, not entirely sure I'm going to be so confident about this come Tuesday.

'You remember where we are – from after the wedding?'

'Yes, Errol Street in North Melbourne, number seventy-three, apartment seventeen.'

'Your dad said you had a thing for numbers.'

'Did he? What time?'

'Any time is fine.'

'Okay, thanks Joy, I'll see you around seven.'

'Oh, Ethan?'

'Yes?'

'I've got something I want to show you.'

'Oh, okay.'

'Bye, Ethan.'

'Bye.'

So I've well and truly smashed my word budget and now I have to wait till Tuesday night to find out what surprise Joy has for me. Terrific.

Laying on the bed and starting in on the familiarity of a number 52 I remember that I've not yet checked on Mister Fantastic. No sign of listing – in fact he looks as happy as a clam, or a tiny fish in his very own ocean.

Outside Travis's spotlights come on.

3. The Levers

How does one prepare for an informal dinner and 'surprise' from a recently inherited step-stranger and her son? The ceiling doesn't have the answer. So I roll onto my side.

I was feeling nostalgic last night so I jerked off to as many nineties icons as I could picture in four and a half minutes. It gave Penelope Cruz a night off. I then slept like a puppy and the morning found me truly relaxed until I realised it was Tuesday and anxiety reversed all the good work.

My view, across a buoyant Mister Fantastic, reminds me that I ate a 52 again last night. Yes, three nights in a row. Well, it ain't a record. A scraping sound comes from beneath the door and my first thought is it's a mouse, meaning the number of souls in this room is increasing for the first time since Mister Fantastic's final friend floated away. I prop myself up on my elbows and, looking over my low-rise stomach – Travis would be proud – see that some mail, okay one letter, has been pushed under the door. Most weekday mornings I hear the same sound over and over, but mostly much fainter. Today the rodent is mine.

I get up, check the weather – looks much like yesterday, which was easily negotiated with a hoodie, say 'Hey' to my stepbrother who hasn't moved – they normally stay plastered a month – and catch up on the news from the street. The banner outside the newsagency tells me that *HOME BUYERS BLOW*. I'm guessing this refers to an interest-rate hike.

The letter is from the fitness centre I recently tired of. All that running was getting me nowhere, just smaller. I open it, expecting them to be pleading with me to get back on the treadmill.

Happy Birthday Ethan – from the team at Fitness First!

Fuck. I'm twenty-seven.

■ ■ ■

The hallway light comes on and through the frosted glass I can see a shadow coming towards the door – a ground-level, street-accessible door named *The Levers*.

It's too tall to be Joy.

'Hey, Ethan, how you doing?'

Travis is, of course, no stranger to me now – he's virtually a flatmate. Even looking at him live he appears Photoshopped. His hair is blond and shoulder-length like in the poster and his eyes really are *that* blue. We have a similar slight build but his stretches way further than mine – like his hair. Though my eyes are green, my blond hair sheared, my skin paler and my stature reduced, I do have *something* on him. About four extra years. However, aside from his obvious greed with sucking up all the best features, we could, at a pinch, be related.

'Not too bad, thanks.'

'How'd you get here?' Travis looks past me to see if I have a car.

'I walked.'

'Ah. Walking,' Travis says, which I don't get what the fuck that means.

All the while he seems to want to chat in the doorway.

'Mum's inside – can you smell that?'

'Um, not sure, what am I smelling?'

'Chicken korma.'

'Cool.'

'Same colour as my shirt.'

I've yet to see dinner, but it may well be.

I follow Travis down the hallway, past three doors on the right and into the open living area, which is one step higher than the kitchen that straddles the far side. The place is very modern – all whites and laminates, lots of windows – and, as I recall from after the wedding, can squeeze in just the number of people required to make a fair amount of noise.

'Mum, Ethan's here.'

Joy stiffly turns her whole body from the stove she's tending, rather than simply swivelling her head. Above surprised black eyebrows her bandana is a bright red colour and she smiles broadly through lips coated the same.

'Hi, Ethan. I'll just remedy this and I'll be with you in barely a sec.'

'No worries.'

Travis points me to the sofa from where I can watch Joy trying to catch up to the korma, and then he, bizarrely, strides to one side of the living area, faces the direction of the far windows, and stands unnaturally erect, contemplating the distance.

'I'm learning to walk,' Travis tells me.

'And I thought I'd taught him that already!' Joy yells out from the kitchen.

'Not like this you didn't,' Travis says and sets off across the room looking determined. His hands are clenched, his arms swing from broad motionless shoulders, but his legwork looks a little bit too Nazi.

Joy turns her entire torso again and smiles kindly before saying, 'Still looks like you're lifting your feet out of wet cement.'

Travis takes the feedback in good spirits and sets himself for a return trip.

Joy has slowed the progress of dinner sufficiently that she has time to watch Travis from the better viewing deck of the sofa.

'I think it's the girls that do the whole show-pony leg-lifts, Trav.'

'I'll try it with a bag.' Travis heads down the hallway, walking like a normal person this time.

Joy turns to me and says, 'Thanks for coming to see us, Ethan,' as if she'd not suggested it.

'Thanks for asking me,' I remind her.

'Last Friday felt so strange and awkward. I didn't know whether to sit in the front row or the back.' Joy looks sad, and for the first time I fully comprehend that she has lost her husband.

Dad met her when they were both diagnosed with aggressive tumours, though for Joy it had been a recurrence, and sent to the same chemotherapy ward. After that he received palliative care in the hospital but Joy did better and was able to go home. Apparently her prognosis is much the same as his but she's somehow handling it all better than he could.

'You know, I wouldn't have minded a bit if you'd sat right there next to me. It was a pretty lonely place,' I tell her, and not just to be polite.

'I'm sitting next to you now,' Joy says, winks, and then hoists herself as elegantly as she can manage off the sofa, 'except I'd better check on dinner.'

Travis returns with an expensive-looking brown-leather bag and, instead of working it across the room, places the closed bag down on the sofa next to me.

'A surprise for you,' Travis says with a smile any photographer would be congratulated on catching.

'Huh?'

'Look inside.'

I peel back the zipper and a little face pops out. It's a chihuahua. This makes me Paris Hilton.

'What's this?'

'It's a doggy bag!' Travis laughs at himself. 'No, this is Diego – he's mine.'

'He's cool,' I say, pulling the chocolate-brown mini-dog out of the bag and resting him on my knee.

Diego shivers like Katharine Hepburn.

'Okay,' Travis says, returning to the side wall with the empty bag. 'Let me try this with a bag this time.'

Joy is starting to ferry bowls, plates and glasses to the table in the centre of the kitchen area.

Travis takes another turn on the catwalk but the bag seems a little superfluous and wobbles about a bit.

'Pretend you've got a bomb in it,' Joy says.

This time Travis looks tougher and more serious. The bag hangs heavy from his arm and he barely lifts his feet whilst pumping his shoulders forward in turn. Joy reckons he's nailed it.

'Tea!' Joy calls and we switch off this fashion channel.

I put Diego onto the sofa to shake some more and we occupy three sides of the table.

'This looks great,' I say honestly.

'Your dad said that you like chicken.'

Huh.

'I used to be a pretty good cook,' Joy says by way of an excuse as we fold the chicken into the rice.

'Still are,' Travis quickly retaliates.

'It might be a bit overdone,' Joy says to me.

'Better than a 52,' I say, and then explain that I'm stuck somewhat in a food rut. The fact that I've been back to the hospital cafeteria since Dad died doesn't faze Joy or Travis. Joy tells me she's sure it's not for the food.

'Is that really all you eat?' Travis asks, without any serious hint of reproach.

'Occasionally I'll have some Maccas.'

'Always the same thing as well?' Travis is actually interested in this dull topic.

'Actually I usually go to a different Maccas each time – I've pretty well tried the whole menu.'

'Looking for something you like?' Travis asks.

'I guess.'

'Why do you go there then?'

I drink some more of the wine I got from up the street on the way here.

'It's stupid really. Dad told me back when I was Diego's age that he thought he saw my mum once. Watching us at a McDonald's. I think he made it up to make me feel better.'

Both Joy and Travis say nothing for a few beats and then Travis says to me, behind his hand, 'So your father knew what your mother looked like?'

Joy makes a 'here we go again' face.

Travis announces, 'Mum was very *popular.*'

'Trav – that's a horrible word,' Joy says but she is only play-acting at indignant.

'So Travis, haven't you actually done catwalk gigs before?' I ask, changing the topic.

'Just photo shoots so far. I'm actually not the most coordinated person in the world.' This is backed up by the fact I count three splashes of korma sauce on his similarly coloured shirt. It'd look worse on white I suppose.

The curry is finished and followed by ice-cream, and we drink much more wine than I arrived with. All the while Travis makes calls on his iPhone but only manages to speak to machines from what I can tell. As he is asking the fourth machine to call him at some point, Joy tells me that she is happy Trav has so many friends.

We talk about work mostly – my lack of it, Joy's time as a waitress, and Travis's many incarnations. Since he left school a halfa-dozen years back he's had just as many jobs. Apparently he has only just started appearing plastered on walls. Immediately prior to that he'd been a charity collector. I ask him if he was one of those street collectors with the forced exuberance of a *Big Brother* contestant. Luckily no – he went door to door. Less street whore – a better class of hooker, he reckons. Before that barman, labouring, waiting on tables – family tradition – and the list goes on.

Travis asks me if I have a dream job and I tell him I don't dream about work.

Just as I'm thinking it's time to go, Joy reminds me she has something she wants to show me.

'I thought maybe you meant Diego.'

But she's already down the hallway seeking out her surprise. I do consider telling them it's my birthday but decide not to.

'Don't you hate machines?' Travis asks out loud, exasperated – I'm the only one about so I'll need to answer.

'I guess.'

Joy returns triumphantly and places what looks like an old school workbook in front of me.

'What's this?'

'It's yours. From Year Five your dad told me,' Joy says, relishing the confusion on my face.

'Wow. It's got my name on the front. He kept this?'

'Sure did. We went through his stuff a few weeks back, when he was up for it. It's all yours of course, but I thought you might like to see this now. I had a look at it with him – I hope you don't mind.'

'Not at all,' I say, flicking through the pages of large pencil writing on unevenly ruled pages.

'Wow, this is a blast. I remember I used to love to write. There must have been a box of these exercise books at one point.'

'My favourite part –' Joy begins.

'You have a favourite part?'

'Yes, we read the entire thing when we discovered it.

'My favourite is the bit where you list what you want when you grow up.' Joy leans over me to guide me through the book.

Travis has given up on contacting his friends via phone, moved to sharing the sofa with the dog and is online, tweeting like a canary.

Upon locating the page she's after, Joy says, 'One more glass of wine I think,' and pours us both as full a glass as is manageable.

The list, my list, seems so foreign, and I'm dumbstruck by me as a ten year old; even more than old photos might make me feel.

'Now, I understand about the pets, and staying up late, and all the lollies you can eat. But what is the first one – Forza Gang?'

Now this I do remember.

'Oh, it's going to sound real dumb now,' I say.

'Not as dumb as my list I'm sure,' Joy says.

'We'll get to *your* list!' I threaten with a smile, my red-wine lips no doubt the colour of Joy's bandana.

'Okay. When I was in upper primary it was all about friends and cliques and at my school they used to have names – the gangs – which also acted as their password. These were not gangs as in hoods or anything, it was just who you sat with or played with – but consistently, without question.'

Joy is immersed in this, which is nice. And I realise I'm more chatty than I can remember. Maybe I need this. And I don't just mean the wine.

'So, anyway, one day – probably just before we were asked to create our wish list – I asked one of the friendlier kids in what seemed to be the coolest of all the gangs what they called themselves and how I might get into a gang. I thought he said their name was Forza Gang – and I was desperate to join Forza Gang and hence the list. Later I discovered he was actually telling me that they had no name – that was the best part – that *four is a gang*. Any four.'

Joy smiles in such a way as to say that this explanation exceeds even her high expectations and she is entirely satisfied. Or she's drunk.

'Now you have to tell me what you would have written forty

years back.' I realise I could have fucked up with my guesstimate of her age but she seems happy with my shot.

Joy nods over to Travis.

'That's one,' she whispers as softly as drunken people can manage.

I smile.

'You know, the only other thing I can think of is travel. I always wanted to travel – even as a hostess. But I ended up being a grounded waitress!'

'Where did you, *do you*, want to go?'

'You were right the first time – I think I'm at *did*,' Joy says, without a hint of self-pity. 'Japan. I think I'd have loved to experience just a bit of its other-worldliness.'

'Fair enough,' I say, feeling a little gloomy all of a sudden, although Joy seems fine with the past tense.

'I'm going to go.' I get up and hug Joy and go over to shake Travis's hand – which is tiring of working his micro key-pad for seemingly not much reward.

'Aren't you forgetting something?' Travis says.

He points at a sleeping Diego.

'No, he's yours,' I say, totally bowled over.

'Yeah but I'm delegating him to you for tonight. Diego has the uncanny knack of sleeping with the person who requires most comfort. I reckon it's your turn.'

With no more discussion Diego is cheerfully packed into Travis's bag and I'm moved down the hallway. I've a suspicion this is their way of ensuring I come back soon, but that's a pretty nice suspicion to deal with.

■ ■ ■

As I walk through the bar at Baxter's with my bag of dog, I get a few looks and I'm guessing they're not wondering if this is a male model but more is it a bomb in there. The entire trip back I found myself daydreaming, which is something I used to do a lot of but haven't for ages. Daydreaming about things ahead – scenarios, options, possibilities. A wish list.

First thing I do is set Diego onto the bed and fetch some water in a bowl. I pull down the window and Diego puts his paws on the windowsill and looks out. He sees Travis and yips recognition.

I check my mobile and there's a missed call. The message is from a lady called Gail Berkus who says she's from The Book Place. Seems I've got an interview. Happy birthday to me.

4. First Impressions

It seemed to make sense to agree to such an early interview slot. It'll show what a morning person I am. The first white lie of what no doubt will be quite a series today. The second being feigning the look of someone comfortable in a suit.

Google told me that The Book Place has over a hundred retail locations nationally and is therefore only eclipsed by its arch nemesis – the grindingly omnipresent mall-chain Books Etcetera: a behemoth no doubt considered by my prospective new colleagues as the evil empire. I also discovered that the buying office for The Book Place chain is just a bunch of blocks down Swanston Street. While this is super appealing, especially this morning, reducing my entire life into one square-kilometre may have its drawbacks for someone attempting to fight off hermititis.

One final check before making a run for it and the mirror shows me that the massive sleep crease across my right cheek is still there – no amount of massaging my face seems to be having any effect. Hopefully Gail Berkus is a Gordon Ramsay fan.

I look with envy at the café just across from The Book Place building before rushing into a lift. Level sixteen is already lit up. Both side walls are supporting a guy each – neither in suits – and I stand in the centre of the space, perfectly equidistant from each of them, to the precise millimetre. As is normal etiquette.

'How was your weekend?' Right-hand-side guy says.

'Not long enough!' Left-hand guy replies with feigned forlorn look.

'You said it.'

Faces down, mine to deflect attention from the fault line running across my cheek and theirs as they've got nothing else to say to each other. We all wear the dour expressions of three guys in an orchestra pit, dragging on violins.

The lift stops on nine and in gets another guy; this one comes to us from the era of under-singlets, combs and handkerchiefs.

'They're new,' the new arrival says proudly. 'I'm breaking them in.'

He thinks we're all checking out his shoes and looks at us all in turn to gauge further interest. I've got nothing.

'How was your weekend?' Right-hand-side guy says.

'Not long enough!' Shoe-guy replies.

'You said it.'

Me and both side-guys get out on sixteen and I follow them into the reception area; immediately I'm hit by the scorched paper smell of an overworked photocopier.

The young guy behind the desk greets the other two.

'How was your weekend?'

'Not long enough!' they say in unison.

'You said it.'

They both head through another door and I linger while the receptionist splays a ream of paper before feeding it into the overworked photocopier.

'How can I help you?'

I want to say 'Not long enough!' but instead, 'I'm here for an 8.45 interview with Gail Berkus.'

'And your name?'

'Ethan Grout.'

The receptionist buzzes through to elsewhere and I hear him leave a message.

'Gail's not at her desk but I've left a message that you're here. I'm sure she'll be out directly. You can take a seat.'

'Thanks,' I say and position myself on a white sofa of real leatherette. I sink – not because it's so soft but rather it feels like it's seen a lot of use. Maybe I'm lucky applicant number 1000. Most of the others had dark hair, and took to lying down, by the look of the equally well-worn cushion that has been flattened into a pancake.

My fists are clenched and it makes me recall Travis's practice runs at walking like a model. Maybe I should employ the same gait in front of Gail when she collects me. Not sure I could pull it off; let's just hope the sleep crease is diminishing.

Various people come through the doors that separate the lift foyer from the reception area before heading through to where the other guys went. Each time the receptionist greets them merrily, and at one point someone calls him James. Whenever it's a woman passing through I uncross my arms and unclench my fists in case it's Gail and she believes in the fine science of body language. But no Gail yet. Most people don't look totally disenchanted with being here, but I try to stave off getting too comfortable with leatherette as the possibility of me getting this job has to be akin to world peace actually being effected by the good offices of Miss Universe.

On the positive side my only other job *was* in a retailer's head office – I assume that's why I got this interview. But it *was* auto parts. There, I said it. If she asks too many questions about books I'm stuffed. I look at the résumé that I've placed into a bright blue plastic sleeve for Gail's bemusement. One page and font size sixteen. Too immature?

A muffled noise seems to be coming from behind what looks like a fire stairwell door that is opposite the bank of lifts in the foyer. I'm about to mention it to James but a couple of blonde girls get out of a lift, hear something as well – move closer to the stairwell door for a better listen and then dismiss it before coming into the reception area, talking to each other all the while.

'I mean when did sushi rolls become the new sandwich?'

'Shut up! Exactly.'

Both girls are cute clichés. The 'Shut up!' girl is completely blonde-gorgeous and the taller one is jam-packed full of oversized features – mouth, boobs and legs. They assess, and reject me, without taking a breath.

'Good morning,' James says, not as fervently as you'd expect.

'Hello, Ecuador,' the taller one replies as blonde-gorgeous swipes them through the door.

Even I know the receptionist's name. He could well be from Ecuador by the look of him but surely his parents didn't name him that.

The next contestant through the reception door is a friendly-looking guy with wet black hair – not gelled wet – water wet – and a towel. James looks at him and asks suspiciously, 'What time did you arrive?'

'Early.'

'How early exactly?'

'Very.'

'Weren't you wearing that on Friday?'

No answer.

The dripping one pulls out his swipe card from a backpack, spills a toothbrush and what looks like a half-loaf of bread onto the floor, scoops it all up and is gone.

James smiles at me and mutters, 'Yeah, like he's been home.'

Maybe this is the place to widen one's world.

And still I reckon I can hear the occasional noise from behind the stairwell door. I'm just about to say something this time when a girl with jet-black shoulder-length hair comes from the lift foyer into reception. She's entirely swathed in black as well – the clothes of the weight conscious. And the stylish. She has her head in a book – *The Art of War*.

'Hey Alejandra!' This time James is completely exuberant.

'Hi James.' Friendly enough but nowhere near as keen as him.

Alejandra starts to search in her bag for her card but James presses a switch from behind his desk, which deactivates the door for her.

'Thank you' she says in a way that leads me to conjecture he may go to this trouble only for her and she realises it with a little awkwardness.

Again with the noise.

'I think I can hear something from that door in the foyer,' I say to Alejandra, who is just about to pass by me.

Alejandra looks at me for the first time and smiles briefly before straining to listen.

'Sounds like Gail,' she says to me and continues on through the security door to elsewhere.

5. Hungry?

James releases Gail Berkus from the fire stairs, though he seemed in no rush when I told him she was in there.

'You must be Ethan,' Gail tells me after emerging from who knows how long in custody.

'Yes. Nice to meet you,' I suggest.

'I like to use the fire stairs between our floors. Bit of exercise. Must remember my security card though!' Gail is explaining why she is a quarter of an hour late, as if I don't know already.

'I imagine you've had the chance to see the team arriving,' Gail says while leading me to a lift. 'Better not take the stairs this time – no need for a card this way.'

We go up just one floor and Gail takes a quick look at my sleep crease when she thinks I'm watching the numbers. I've already stolen my peek at her – she's stolen Aung San Suu Kyi's serene glow and her ponytail, which she wears grey. Gail has no earlobes whatsoever.

'On this level we have some meeting rooms, the kitchen, and other facilities for the team,' Gail says proudly, leading me between two rows of meeting rooms. They're all indistinguishable from each other save for the names on the doors. Each room is named after a book, she tells me.

'We're in Twilight,' Gail says, holding the door open and pointing out which chair I'm to sit in. This room is in the central part of the building so no window. I'm losing track of time.

Gail takes the chair opposite me and I remind myself to remove my elbows from the table that separates us.

'Let's get started,' Gail says and then looks at me expectantly as if this is my meeting.

'Um. I should give you this,' I say, handing over the single-page résumé.

'Big font.'

'Thanks.'

Why did I just say 'thanks'?

'So, Ethan, you were at Auto World for nine years?'

'And a bit.'

As if the bit matters.

'Tell me why you left Auto World?'

'I needed a change.'

This answer is true. Though a little short, so I try to fill the silence with puff.

'I'd achieved everything I wanted to there and am keen for a fresh challenge.'

Now I'm definitely straying into fiction. Time to deflect.

'I'm keen to hear more about The Book Place.'

'Well, we have a great team,' I think tears are forming in her eyes, 'and great stores out there.' She points in the direction of the outside world.

'Our number-one goal is to remain number two,' Gail adds triumphantly.

'And my role would be –'

Gail cuts me off. 'Your role would be as part of my team, of course. Each person in my team …'

This is the fifth time she's said the word 'team'. When did everybody form into teams? Where was I?

'... has a particular book category and ensures that they've ordered new releases in that category in the right quantity for each of our locations.'

'Sounds great,' I say, though I'm already starting to fear the inevitable questions about what titles I've read and my favourite authors – but they never come. In fact, Gail seems to downplay the importance of the actual books themselves. It's all a numbers game, she reckons – no need to get caught up in the publishers' hype about the writers or the marketing and publicity plans. Books are no different to exhaust pipes she says. That seems entirely odd but it works nicely in my favour.

Now that Gail is talking there's no stopping her and I just let her go for it. She explains the structure of the company: they have a marketing *team* that we in the buying *team* need to keep in the loop so they know which new books to feature in advertising, catalogues and in the stores; and a merchandising *team* that looks after keeping stock levels right and positioning in the stores.

'Just like Auto World,' I say – which Gail soaks up.

My stomach rumbles and Gail thinks her mobile is vibrating, and then eventually remembers she doesn't have it with her.

'The three teams are encouraged to mix though,' she assures me. 'We have lots of bonding activities, and the other two managers and I ensure we blend everybody together. We need to have fun together. It's essential.'

'Sounds great.'

I'm repeating myself but Gail doesn't seem to be bothered.

'Ethan,' serious face from Gail, 'tell me what interests you? How do you spend your spare time?'

'I like movies, um, I quite like walking. Writing – yes, writing.'

I leave out daydreaming, masturbation and eating alone.

'That's fine ...' Gail says.

'Thank you,' I say too quickly.

'... but they're all solitary pursuits.'

Shit. An amateur psychologist.

'What about activities that involve a group. Any interests there, Ethan?'

'Yes.'

Gail nods at me, trying to elicit more.

'Yes. I'd like to be part of a group.'

'I think we should do the test,' Gail says to me and my empty stomach drops.

'Test?'

'We give all applicants our standard test. I'll go get someone from human resources and they'll take you through it.'

I could easily just get up and leave – no test questions asked. But before that idea can fully take root Gail returns with a young guy.

'Ethan, this is Beckham Ang. Beckham Ang is in the human resources team.'

I'm not sure why she uses his full name, especially when he'd selected a memorable first name after tiring of spelling his Chinese one to guilos.

'Hi Ethan. This won't hurt,' Beckham Ang jokes, placing a test paper in front of me as Gail wanders off.

Beckham Ang explains the test and tells me I have half an hour to do as many multiple-choice questions as I can manage. For an HR person he's very friendly, unlike the puppets of the regime at Auto World. Beckham Ang assures me that he got his job here after barely answering half the questions, then sets his watch and is off.

I quickly jump up and cross the hallway, entering an empty office that has a window and check the sun. It's just after ten.

As luck would have it an inordinate number of questions are simply about selecting the number that comes next in a particular sequence. The answers jump into my head like daydreams and in the space between two stomach rumbles I've sorted out all the number pattern questions and start on the remaining ones that are mostly about unjumbling sentences. Words are more difficult and before I'm done with these Beckham Ang returns.

'And time's up!' he announces, collects my paper and tells me he'll send Gail back in.

'How do you feel you went?' Gail asks me on returning to the meeting room.

'Pretty good I think.'

'Well, thanks for coming in to see us. Once we've had a chance to analyse your results I'll be in contact. Have you any more questions?'

'No, I think you've explained everything.'

'So, Ethan, are you *hungry?*' Gail looks me square in the eye.

She's either realised *that* sound is my stomach or, more bizarrely, she's asking me to lunch.

'I am actually.' No eating alone today. 'Starving in fact.'

'Great,' Gail says. 'We only want team members who are *really* hungry!'

Oh.

6. Solitary Pursuits

Under the sun again and I feel in serious need of some recharging. Walking back along Swanston, I already feel done with this day while most of the cafés around me are still serving breakfast – to my fellow footloose colleagues. Throughout the first Sausage McMuffin I contemplate the possibility that the job at The Book Place merely entails completing number patterns. Not likely. Maybe making me do a test was simply Gail's payback for leaving her too long on the fire stairs.

My second McMuffin is accompanied by a broader selection of daydreams. Now that I'm back into scenario-musing I can't imagine what I'd done without this excellent method for passing empty time.

I run back through my morning and, although the clock above the town hall had not moved for the duration, something has changed. The fact is, I *actually* want this job. However, are the folk that drifted through the foyer – my possible new work buddies – any more likely to pitch in more than a handful of coins each when I've done near on ten years with them than the last lot? I came away from that sterile decade with nothing, no one, to show for it.

An old guy with less hair than Golem sits next to a lady with breasts so large they rest on our window bench – enabling his coffee to warm her nipples. The guy tells his woman about this morning's news and overnight developments in Iran. She reminds him it's bin night.

My dad would be proud of me at least trying for a different job – can't tell him now though. If my mother was at this Maccas – she's not, I checked already – I doubt her level of interest would exceed zero.

Suddenly the thought occurs to me – to travel back in time and write a letter. I should write Joy a letter and thank her for dinner the other night. When I returned Diego the next day she wasn't there and who knows if Travis would have remembered to tell her how much I'd enjoyed a home-cooked meal. A home. I might also mention my job interview.

After buying a pad and a pen from the newsagent that's running with *BALI BELLY!* as the day's big news – apparently Mariah Carey is on holiday in Indonesia and may be pregnant (or more likely just stuffed on satays) – I secure one of those metallic green outdoor benches that would burn my flesh if it were summer *and* I weren't wearing a suit.

The letter starts with a respectable number of sentences appreciating the invite, the food and the chihuahua. And then it's me on me: I tell Joy about the interview and about missing my dad. Then I write that I hope she does get to Japan – at least gets a taste of it. Choosing the words for that bit was like fishing with chopsticks. I mean, I told Gail I like to write, that is I used to, but it doesn't mean I'm any good at it however. Luckily I have a whole pad of paper for rewrites.

It's quite a distance – to deliver the letter – but why pay a postman to do your walking in the sunshine?

I walk virtually the length of Swanston, strolling like the unemployed, all the way to Melbourne Uni, and then take Grattan, past the hospitals – where I easily ignore the cafeteria's call – and into North Melbourne. There is a new Maccas along the way but I'm too full to do anything more than quickly scan the faces of the middle-aged women inside.

Sat on the single step outside the door called *The Levers* there *is* in fact a middle-aged woman. I presume she is a friend of Joy's and smile as I lean past her and slip the letter under the door, and from what it sounds like straight into Diego's mouth.

'He's not home,' the lady says forlornly.

She looks a bit old to be a Travis groupie.

'Oh, the letter is for Joy,' I say.

'Do you know Travis?' she asks.

'Yes. He's my stepbrother actually.' That's the first time I've said it out loud. 'How do you know him?'

'We met when he was collecting for charity. I was on his route.'

I leave her perched there and start back to the city. Hopefully Diego won't chew the letter too badly and the step-sitter doesn't waste too much time waiting on my stepbrother.

■ ■ ■

'Good Luck. What your order?'

'Number 52, please?'

'Name?'

'Ethan.'

'Ten minutes.'

'Thanks.'

Before collecting my dinner, I decide to quickly cruise the DVD store and rent as many of the movies that I had to ditch when they couldn't be squeezed out of the limp gift card I got from Auto World. There is more than one way to skin that cat.

'Hi. Takeaway to collect.'

'Name?'

'Ethan.'

Never once have they acknowledged that they've seen me before. Am I a ghost? The benefit to being a ghost is you can clothes shop undisturbed or use a bar's facilities without buying a drink. Maybe I'm just too pale.

I fuck around with my money as if the price of this dish is a total surprise to me. Zhen, who at least has the sense to wear his name plastered to his chest, accepts the coins and doesn't suggest he'll see me again soon.

As Mister Fantastic, a now peeling Travis and I settle into our regular positions to view the first movie, and I'm just about to down the first mouthful of 52, my mobile rings.

Unknown.

'Hello?'

'Hi Ethan, this is Gail Berkus. Gail Berkus from The Book Place.'

Oh, *that* Gail Berkus.

'Hi,' I say, waiting for the letdown.

'Ethan, I am very pleased to offer you the role as a book buyer with my team!'

'Really? I mean great!'

How can this be? Were there no other applicants?

As if reading my mind Gail says, 'Your results in the test were very solid. As I mentioned in the interview we are after a *numbers* guy. Not someone too *booky* – a head for processes.'

Maybe the fact that I've no experience with books is exactly what she's looking for. She won't be the first boss who prefers to have people with far less to offer beneath them. And thus, I'm perfect.

'So, Ethan, what do you say?'

So, Ethan, what *do* you say? I'd forgotten this was an offer rather than a gift.

'Yes! Of course, thanks.'

'You really do sound like you're starving! Welcome on board!'

Toot. Toot.

7. Ethan Takes a Job

'How was your weekend?'

'Too long,' I say.

The guy looks at me as if to say, *You must* never *stray from the script*.

It is pointless to hope his dark good looks and angular jaw – which necessitated the creation of the swivelling razorblade – will be getting off at a different floor as we are both staring at a sole light, behind the number sixteen, wishing it to somehow ignite any of the others.

I follow Prince Charming through the foyer and James, the receptionist I met last week at my interview, is already replying, 'Yeah, not long enough, Mitch.'

'You said it!' And all is right again in Mitch's world.

After Mitch marches through I greet James and he is amazed I recall his name. He wouldn't be if he knew how few names get thrown at me any given week.

'I'd introduce you around but I've been instructed to immediately record all the serial numbers on our office equipment,' James says. 'I'll get the Hamster to show you about.'

'The Hamster?'

'Yes, she's the assistant to the three book managers – Gail for buying, Penny for merchandising, and you just saw Mitch. He's marketing.'

James buzzes through and then announces to me, 'She's on her way.'

'I guess I'd better know – you know – her real name?'

'It's Rachel,' James replies. 'Rachel the Hamster.'

The Hamster is, in fact, no bigger than a gerbil. She must, looking up at me, feel like I do with Travis. She has short, and yes, mousy brown hair. Her glossy pink lipstick has strayed a little beyond the lip line. All that said, I immediately sense a toughness and strength that betrays her stature. Her expression is confident and her manner direct.

'Hello Ethan. Let's do the tour,' Rachel says after shaking my hand with the strength of someone twice her size.

Before getting through the security door we have to negotiate our way around the skinny guy I saw last week as I waited for someone to care enough to release my appointment from the fire stairs. The guy who looked like he'd just stepped out of the shower.

'Dale, did you leave that pizza box upstairs? In the kitchen?' Rachel asks accusingly.

'Yes.'

'It stinks – get rid of it. Don't treat this place like your home.' Rachel the Hamster says this with the glint of a sinister smile. Could she have a gold molar?

We leave a broken Dale, who heads back to the lifts and up to level seventeen where, the Hamster nicely segues into explaining, there is the kitchen and lunchroom, showers and amenities, meeting rooms and boardroom, and *ancillary* departments like human resources.

'So, we can tick Dale off,' the Hamster makes it sound like we're going to be pushing through the office and picking off the team with a gun, 'as having been met.'

'Dale is in the marketing team. Well it's just him and his manager, Mitch, actually. Small team,' she muses, before letting me through security and into the vastness of the main floor.

I look to my left and there lies a football field of cluttered office furniture – with people fossicking through it as if at a tip. I'd already forgotten what working looked like.

Down the left side of the vast space is the passageway that allows you to enter the maze on the right at whichever juncture takes your fancy. Within the maze most of the desk arrangements are pod-style – three people per pod, each looking inward to the pod's centre. The internal sides of each pod's three equal segments are framed by flimsy felt-covered barriers, low enough so you can communicate to your pod-colleagues without meerkating too awkwardly. I can see many of the barriers have photos of loved ones pinned to them, as you'd expect to see on the walls of a prison cell.

Here we go …

As we commence the trek down the passageway, passing the teams the Hamster has already determined are too ancillary for me to meet, the computer screens of the row of people facing the passageway click over from colourful Facebook pages to something more businesslike, one by one, with the precise timing of a line of tumbling dominos.

At the halfway line we turn into the maze and stop, facing two pods. Seated at one pod are the two blonde girls I saw the other day, and at the other pod is the girl I'd alerted about the noise in the stairwell – Alejandra – and another I don't recognise. Each pod has an empty chair.

'Attention. I'll introduce you all at once,' the Hamster says, clapping her paws and getting quite a sound out of them.

Alejandra and one of the blonde girls have to peer up, over the barriers, whilst the other two simply swivel in their chairs.

I can feel myself start to redden simply through the pressure of trying not to. It's been a while since I've had more than one set of eyes upon me.

'Everybody, this is Ethan. He is the new fiction buyer.'

Everybody says nothing.

Pointing at the blonde pod the Hamster says, 'This is Ingrid – she is the nonfiction buyer – and this is *Brhe* …' The Hamster pronounces this second name very sceptically, as if this is how blonde number two *claims* her name is pronounced. '… B. R. *H.* E. – the buyer for kids' books.'

'You'll sit here,' the Hamster adds, pointing at the empty chair in Pod Blonde.

'And over here we have the merchandising team – Alejandra and Lillian.' Lillian is plain-looking, a bit older than Alejandra, who I'm guessing is looking thirty square in the eyes. And while Lillian's hair is too dark to qualify for my pod, it's not a patch on Alejandra's. Both Lillian and Alejandra give me more acknowledgment than my pod-buddies.

'Penny, the merchandising manager, is also in the process of hiring a third team member,' the Hamster informs me, acknowledging they have an empty chair as well.

I'm left standing for a few unsettling moments before the Hamster says, 'Now we'll go meet the team managers.'

At the far end of the field, larger desks face out over the view of the city. I recognise Gail and she swivels around welcomingly.

'I hope Rachel has been looking after you.'

Who's Rachel? Oh, that's right.

'Yes,' I say, smiling appreciatively at the Hamster.

'I'll leave you then,' says the Hamster and she's back up along the side of the maze.

'Ethan, this is Penny,' Gail says, presenting the older lady, with silver-rimmed glasses and the eyebrows more usually associated with testosterone, sitting next to her.

Penny's desk is festooned with Brazilian flags.

'Hello Ethan. That's a nice name. What's your background?'

'Keilor East.'

'And this is Mitch, the marketing manager.' Gail swivels to her other side. Mitch is on the phone, thank fuck.

'Yes, I met him in the lift this morning,' I say to Gail so she doesn't feel the need to interrupt him.

Gail drags a chair from an empty pod space nearby and I sit down facing her.

'Well, you've certainly started at a busy time, Ethan,' she tells me.

'Sure have!' Penny says, spinning in such a way as to say she wants to be included, but Gail gives her a look in such a way as to say she's not.

'This week we are seeing all the large book publishers with their presentations of their lead titles for Christmas.'

'Christmas? As in not-for-ages Christmas?'

Gail nods. 'We need to get our orders in as early as possible so they print what we want and we don't miss out.'

Suddenly the fun of meeting a fresh slew of people is being submerged by the enormity of the fact I'm completely out of my depth here. I want this job but at the same time don't want *a* job. Is this what an impending mortgage feels like? Or marriage? When do I get to play with the number patterns?

The look of fear on my face must be apparent to Gail, who I recall at the interview didn't seem particularly bothered by my lack of book experience. 'Don't worry,' she assures me, 'the merchandisers are here to work with us on getting the order quantities right.'

'Oh, that's good.'

'So, tomorrow and the next day we have the presentations, and then on Thursday we all get together with marketing and plan out our promotions for the Christmas period, bearing in mind the books we've just seen.'

'Makes sense,' I say, partway truthfully.

'And then on Friday it's bonding day!' Gail announces proudly.

'Bonding day?'

'It's mostly a surprise so you'll just have to wait till then.' Gail is abuzz with the thrill of it all and even Penny wants to add to the cheer, but Gail has locked her into staring straight ahead, her knees jammed against Penny's chair.

There is a long way to go until Friday and if I make it to the end of the week I might be just as excited as these two.

All the while I can hear Marketing Mitch in the background, talking to designers, and agencies, and whoever else – one after the other – talking about needing to add 'his build to that' and requesting they come up with a better 'call to action'.

'I'll walk you back to your desk, you need to complete these payroll forms.' Gail hands me some papers and motions for me to follow her. However, instead of going up the passageway we walk straight ahead and Gail knocks on the door of what looks like a windowless internal office. The door has a lock that can be activated with a code – maybe it's the stationery stash.

'The server room. IT,' Gail whispers, as if we're entering a morgue. 'No one likes to go in here – it's so cold and lifeless.'

An Indian guy opens the door as if he never gets visitors. I recognise the expression.

He lets us by reluctantly and once inside Gail introduces me to him – Alex – and to another Indian guy, this one with the headdress of a Sikh. Sachin.

'Alex and Sachin keep us all wired,' Gail says, trying to sound hip.

'Guys, this is Ethan – the new member of the buying team. I just wanted to check that you've set up his computer and email address and everything else you do?'

'All done,' Alex says. 'Your initial password is "help". For anyone's email just start typing their full name and it will automatically convert it to our address format. We'll get you a security card by the end of the day.'

'Thanks,' I say, and we leave the chill of the morgue.

Gail deposits me at my desk with my forms and I find a pen, sitting atop my keyboard, the interior of which is filled with crumbs and sesame seeds. I start filling in the details so if I do last a week here at least I'll get paid for it. Neither Ingrid nor Brhe looks at me so far as I can tell, and I take my time as once I've done with this chore I'm clueless about what to do next. Listening in to these two natter away to each other is unfulfilling – they both use the word 'apparently' with the regularity of the worst of gossips and from what I can ascertain, refer to most of their office colleagues by country of origin rather than actual name.

I peer over my left-hand side partition to Ingrid, the taller of the blondes.

'Excuse me. What should I do with these forms?'

'You need to take them up to Bang.'

I haven't a fucking idea what that means.

'Shut up Ingrid! How would he know who Bang is?' Brhe steps in.

'Beckham Ang – human resources – our email formats his name to Bang. When you type Beckham you get Bang. Bang at the book place,' Brhe tells me. She seems the nicer one of these, apparently inseparable, Olsen twins.

I recall Beckham Ang – he gave me the test, the results of which so disoriented Gail that she offered me this job.

Planning to discover the HR offices on level seventeen by myself, I get up to wander towards the lifts but Brhe says to me, 'We've got the Monday meeting now.'

'Oh. Do I need to bring anything?'

'Glee,' a voice behind me says. 'It's mandatory.'

Alejandra smiles at me but seems in no rush to move.

Everybody from the floor traipses towards the foyer of lifts and starts gliding up to seventeen in shifts. Some people take the fire stairs but as I've not yet got a security card I'm not going to attempt that. Inside the lift I'm lucky to secure a spot in, Ingrid leans past me and whispers into Brhe's ear, 'Is Mexico coming?'

'Not sure. She didn't look like she was getting up.'

'What about Algeria?'

'Don't know.'

'Data junkies,' Ingrid mutters, exasperated.

'Merchandisers,' Brhe says to me by way of explanation.

Ingrid leans in to the both of us as the lift comes to a stop and says, 'Penny only hires third-worlders.'

'Shut up!'

I wish it was me who said that, but it was Brhe. And unfortunately she said it in the supportive way.

■ ■ ■

'There's more room up the front. Don't be shy.' Penny seems to be running the meeting, with Beckham Ang from HR and a guy who appears to be his manager. We are in a massive meeting room without windows, so I've no idea what the time is, but from most of the faces I'd say it's not fun time.

Most people are leaning against the three walls whilst facing those up front, but some have sat on the floor like kindergarteners. James the receptionist, Alex and Sachin from IT, and Rachel the Hamster all sit on crossed legs as if their backs are made of rubber. Dale, however, is sprawled out amongst them like he's about to nod off.

'It's my turn today to lead us through the agenda. It shouldn't take long as we've just a few items that we need reminding on before we can get into the week!' Penny says, beaming with the power.

'First up – a reminder that Friday is a surprise treat for all of us and the only clue to the day's activity is the dress code – posh!'

Enough groans ensue to suggest that there are plenty of members of the resistance amongst this rally.

'Second item – more fun! We need a name for this room to help us differentiate it from the other, more *intimate* meeting rooms. As you know those are named with book titles, but we'd like to give this large room a name that encompasses its role as the place where we all come together to share ideas and dreams. All suggestions welcome!'

'The room with no name.'

'We need a name,' Penny says to the entire gathering, unsure who called that out.

'But that is a name – "The room with no name". That's the name.'

It's a guy on the far wall, for whom I've no name as yet.

Beckham Ang's manager steps in to quell the dissent. 'No, that's merely a *suggestion*.'

'Any more suggestions?' Beckham Ang's manager asks as Penny steps back, leaving the meeting to him.

'The United Nations.'

It's Ingrid.

Penny likes it. She believes Ingrid is being nice.

'Let's think some more. Email your ideas to Beckham Ang.' Beckham Ang's manager refers to his sidekick by his full name as well.

Beckham Ang steps forward after a nod from his manager.

'Birthdays and anniversaries,' he announces.

I've no room for more names so allow them to wash over me, these people turning older in the week ahead or celebrating a certain number of years' service at The Book Place. We applaud them as if they're here but not a single one of the celebrated people seems to have attended the meeting. Various colleagues call out 'on leave' or 'running late' after each name. Maybe that's why we applaud them. Beckham Ang shifts a few steps sideway, as if trying to distance himself from his leader, who again takes charge.

'Finally a few reminders regarding the dress code and punctuality.'

Groans.

'You all know the dress code – if you don't, do not look at the person next to you but ask your manager. Or you can ask Beckham Ang who will gladly assess what you are wearing – for a verdict on whether or not it fits into our code.'

Beckham Ang is busy studying his shoes.

They dragged us all up here for this?

'Now, let's talk about punctuality. The day starts at eight-thirty and ends no sooner than five.'

Someone sticks an elbow into Dale's ribs and he yelps like a puppy and turns bright red. A bright red puppy that appears to have slept in his clothes.

'As you know, we like people to take lunch around twelve-thirty – this helps with bonding between teams.'

'But if you're late for work or leave early or your lunch break goes over, then it must be made up,' Beckham Ang's manager continues.

'Should we keep a record of minutes late, tally up and make them up on weekends or a particular night each week?'

I look down the wall I'm helping to hold up, toward the door, and see Alejandra. She did make it to the meeting. Alejandra wears a straight face for Beckham Ang's manager's benefit.

'I'm not sure that is necessary, Alejandra. We are all adults and we like to treat you as adults.'

'Can we get a credit for time spent in the lift or do we measure from the time we arrive in the foyer?'

'If you need guidance, then let's say from the time you swipe your security card.'

He is taking her seriously. Ingrid doesn't get it. The Hamster could kill.

'What if the lift is full and it takes two minutes to deliver everyone – that doesn't seem fair?

'Alejandra, I think you should take up the details with Beckham Ang. We've all got a job to do and this meeting has gone long enough. Thanks, everyone, for all your input and have a great and profitable week ahead.'

Meeting over.

8. Lunch Bonding 101

The indiscriminate nature of my introductions means I'm not entirely sure who I have and haven't met yet. So now, to avoid embarrassment or apparent rudeness, I need to nod knowingly at everyone I run into. After the morning meeting Ingrid was nominated by Gail to continue parading me around the office; she did her best with the names but often resorted to whispering to me, after the handshake and stilted conversations, which country the person I'd just met came from. Then I was deposited back at my desk to go through the notes my predecessor had left. They read like a goodbye and good luck letter from someone actually being released from Guantanamo Bay.

The café directly across the road is full of lanyarded people and I'm mostly clueless as to which ones are from The Book Place and smile a half-hello to anyone who looks my way, lest I'm accused of blanking a new colleague.

With a takeaway that resembles 52, I make my way back to the building and then to level seventeen for the enforced bonding known as lunchtime.

The lunchroom is a big space, again without windows, which has a kitchen at one end and an entertainment centre at the other, closest to the door. In the centre of the room is the massive communal table – that aims, presumably, to bring all the diners together as one corporate family.

Alex, Sachin and Dale have all forsaken food and conversation for Wii. Ingrid and Brhe sit at the very centre of the long table, facing each other, and are sharing a big bowl of what appears to be vegetable dumplings. Lillian sits next to Brhe. There is a random selection of five other people, the names and homelands of whom I'm not sure I've been introduced to yet. I smile at them all, for little reward, before skulking into the kitchen to seek out some soy sauce.

After putting my takeaway container onto the cleanest part of a bench that's awash with crumb-laden toast sweat, I'm approached by the beaming face of Penny – or Kofi Annan as Ingrid would have her. Alejandra's with her – looking for cutlery to excavate her turkey salad.

'Ethan – have you met Alejandra yet?' Penny says.

And before I can answer Penny adds triumphantly, 'She's from Mexico!'

I look at Alejandra. She has the most beautiful brown eyes and rich caramel skin.

'My stepmother has a chihuahua,' I announce.

What the fuck is that!

Alejandra looks at me and says flatly, 'Aye caramba.'

My face is so fired I could heat my lunch up on it.

Alejandra goes over to the table and sits the same side of the table as Ingrid, leaving an empty space between them. Penny wanders off as happily as ever.

Where the fuck am I going to sit now? Do I try to explain that I'm a moron? I guess she knows that already.

Meekly making my way over to the table, I try to decide which seat allows me to make the least statement. I sit next to Lillian but one, roughly across, though not directly, from Alejandra. This allows me to vaguely make out that I'm watching Dale slaughter both Alex and Sachin in turn at Wii tennis, while being on hand to pick up on any conversation openings that might give me a smooth entrée into the lunch team.

■ ■ ■

'… if I hear more about that movie I'll scream.' Ingrid to Brhe.

Dale serves to Sachin. An ace.

'Shut up! It's usually me who gets caught listening to him go on and on about it! Watch something else, you boring codger!' All those exclamation points – definitely Brhe to Ingrid.

'Who is that?' Lillian asks, wanting to play.

'The old guy next door to us,' Brhe replies with a soft shot.

So Ingrid and Brhe live together as well. Huh.

'You do realise that World War II is actually a war, not a film?' That's Alejandra with a flat serve.

The silence that ensues means they didn't. Shit – and Ingrid is the nonfiction buyer. No need to worry about my lack of experience then.

Ingrid and Brhe settle back into dipping their forks alternately into the bowl in the centre of the table and returning a dumpling to their empty heads. I take the opportunity to swivel my neck, like Gail in her chair, and join in with the table a bit more.

'Don't you think Dale looks a bit like that guy from "Amish and Handy"?' Brhe whispers to a munching Ingrid.

'It's *Hamish* and *Andy*,' Ingrid replies as Brhe takes her turn to dip.

'Really?'

'Really.' Even Ingrid's made incredulous by her BFF.

'Well, whatever, he looks a bit like him,' Brhe says.

'I *love* Hamish!' Ingrid says. 'Dale looks like Andy.'

Lillian, a little slow to learn her lesson, tries to join in again. 'I think inner beauty is more important than physical looks.'

'You would though, wouldn't you,' Ingrid says.

I look over at Alejandra and her eyes are up to the ceiling. She must sense me looking at her and she smiles over the table at me.

'So, what's this chihuahua's name then? Pepe?'

'No. Diego.'

'That's my little brother's name.'

'Oh. Sorry.'

How can this keep happening?

'No, that's okay; actually Diego's the mongrel of our litter.' Alejandra smiles wryly and lets me off the stupid hook.

Brhe has left the room so Ingrid is stuck talking to Lillian. And vice versa. Apparently Ingrid just got a new puppy and she's explaining how decrepit the lady she bought it from was.

'How old was she?' Lillian asks.

'Very.'

'How old is the puppy?'

'Ten weeks.'

'Will you have to train him?'

'I trained him to sit on the weekend!' Ingrid boasts.

'He's been standing all this time?' Alejandra joins in, straight-faced.

We both laugh, but Ingrid directs her scorn towards Mexico.

'I guess you don't care much for animals,' Ingrid says.

'I love animals,' Alejandra replies.

'How can *you* be an animal lover when *you* eat meat?'

'That's what I love about them.'

Just at that moment Ingrid loses the final dumpling off her fork and it hits the table. Before she has a chance to collect it, another fork stabs into it. Alejandra eats the dumpling, gets up and leaves the lunchroom.

Ingrid stares at me as if to say, *Can you believe her?* Then finally says, 'Can you believe her?'

Maybe it's too early to join teams but I'm not liking the look of Ingrid's.

Brhe returns with a scoop for her flatmate. 'I just saw Penny leading some chick off to interview for the spare merchandiser role!'

'What does she look like?' Ingrid asks.

'Sort of like Mexico. But fatter.'

Beckham Ang walks in and reminds us, as if he's been forced to, that lunchtime is limited, so everybody sets about heading back to their desks. I feel like protesting that if they wanted us to keep track of time, a few windows would be nice, but realise Beckham Ang is not the problem. Moreover, I've had enough bonding for the day.

Tomorrow I buy books. With this lot.

9. Christmas Come Early

'Stalin was a spunk.'

'Shut up!'

Ingrid and Brhe are enjoying the Christmas titles presentation from the rep for a publisher called Tate Lane.

The image on the screen of the upcoming biography of Stalin as a young man certainly paints him in a fine light and, until the rep chanted his accompanying short blurb on Stalin's place in history, Ingrid, our nonfiction buyer, had apparently thought him a movie icon from the thirties.

We are well into the second presentation and over the next two days have around ten to get through. The pattern seems to be – start off with Penny's *fun* quick quiz for the rep – to make him or her feel entirely uncomfortable, under the guise of making everyone feel comfortable and familiar; a run-through of sales figures for the past year; the presentation of the lead titles by the rep; and finally a postmortem once the rep has left in which we can speak our minds and discuss tentative buying quantities.

The next jacket image comes up. Castro. This should be interesting.

'Isn't he dead yet?' At least Ingrid knows who is – probably the title being *Castro: A Life* has clued her in as to who is wearing the beard.

'No. But he is *very* sick!' the rep replies merrily. It is Christmas after all.

'Let us know when he does drop,' Ingrid says.

'I'm sure it'll be all over the net,' the rep says.

'Even hotornot.com?' Alejandra, next to me, says just loud enough to delight me, and Lillian on her other side.

Alejandra is looking typically festive – all black. Whereas Lillian has gone with a more traditional green. It is swathed over her in the construct of a cape – only she could explain what that's about.

Ingrid and Brhe preside over the other side of the boardroom table, whilst at the head, directly facing the screen and the bemused rep standing by it, are Gail and Penny, separated by a humourless hamster.

The rep clicks for the next slide and it appears to be an autobiography for the young adult section – imaginatively titled *Zac Efron: A Life*.

'Ker-ching!' Gail calls out. This is not the first time today she's done that. The first time I covered my face, fearing it was a spray of swine flu.

Brhe, the kids' buyer, starts spending her bonus cheque immediately: massive plasma, pink BlackBerry, massive boobs, Miss Tizzy fashions and cubicle with porthole on P&O's *Sea Princess*.

'I've got a couple of promotional T-shirts for our Christmas campaign if anyone wants them,' the Tate Lane rep says in a not particularly enthusiastic way. Presumably they're crap.

He holds the T-shirts out as if they're covered in shit and Ingrid swipes at them first.

'Oh, they're large,' Ingrid says, tossing them on the table in front of Alejandra.

Alejandra casually picks them off the table, swivels in her chair and drops them into a bin.

After the rep is released from hell, Gail leads us on a run-through of what we've just seen.

'Ingrid, what number did you have in mind for the Princess Mary biog?'

'I'm not sure – I'll get Mexico to check previous sales.'

'There are no previous sales – this is the first one,' Alejandra states.

'I'm sure we can find a similar book to compare it to,' Gail says.

'Check how many we sold of the Princess Diana biographies,' Ingrid instructs Alejandra.

'Do you think they're comparable? Princess Mary is Australian. Maybe this book has no precedent,' Alejandra says.

'There has to be a precedent,' says Gail.

'Delta Goodrem?' Brhe helps out.

'Judith Lucy – that went well – check the numbers for that. I'm sure we could do the same,' Gail, the precedent junkie, decides.

'*¿Porqué no?*' Alejandra asks herself, looking around the room with the expression of a freshly landed alien.

'Ker-ching!' I whisper and, for a moment, she looks a little less stranded.

■ ■ ■

'We're getting 4G set up tonight!' Ingrid is boasting in the lunchroom to Lillian. She is talking to Lillian because Brhe has disappeared.

'What's 4G?' Lillian asks.

'It's the next step on from 3G,' Ingrid says.

'What's 3G?'

'I don't know.'

'How will you set it up?'

'There's an Indian guy living on our floor so I asked him.'

Brhe comes into the lunchroom, proudly leading a former colleague doing the whole 'I had a baby' thing.

Most of the diners know the woman and make a fuss over the wrapped parcel in her sling. The mother is afforded centre-of-table status and we eat our lunch around her as she tells us the kid's daily routine, between incoming messages on the apparatus glued to her hand. Baby's first word is likely to be 'iPhone'.

'My entire world has been turned upside down. I never fully realised how insignificant my life had been – before I became a mum!'

Then, 'So, what have you all been up to?'

Various people offer up their tidbits of news and supermum looks a little underwhelmed. She turns to Alejandra who is poking at her salad.

'How's Damien?'

'He's fine.'

'Is Ecuador still following you about like a puppy?'

Alejandra says nothing.

'Shut up! Like ever!' Brhe answers for Alejandra.

Brhe might have taken a break from talking but this doesn't necessarily mean she's been thinking.

'Come on, Alejandra, give me something!' the woman says in mock exasperation at Alejandra's reluctance to open up.

'Um. I have been obsessing about pancakes with maple syrup a lot ...'

'Best not,' Ingrid whispers under her breath and the woman grins.

'... it feels like I'm pregnant,' Alejandra says.

'You've no idea what it feels like to be pregnant!' The woman draws a line between those who've lived the dream and those who haven't.

'I don't know – I know what it feels like to be fat,' Alejandra replies.

The woman forges on. 'Don't you want to have kids?'

'I can barely entertain myself,' Alejandra says, then, 'I'm going out for some fresh air.'

I've already worked out that this, ironically, is code for a ciggie break.

Alejandra leaves the lunchroom and now the postmortem will be about her.

'Mexico still looks good, *I suppose,* but her attitude!' the woman says to Ingrid and Brhe.

'She might have been hot five and ten ago, I guess,' Ingrid says.

'Five and ten?' Lillian asks.

'Years and kilos.'

The conversation goes round and round but I'm too busy wondering who Damien is to listen in. I realise suddenly that I don't want it to be Alejandra's husband or boyfriend, though I'll concede it's a rather ordinary name for a pet.

'So, what are you all doing this week?' the visitor asks whilst whipping out a breast for the parcel to nuzzle.

'We've got Christmas presentations today and tomorrow, marketing Thursday, and some bonding-day surprise on Friday,' Brhe says.

'Oh, we've also got "shave your hair for leukemia day" tomorrow,' Lillian chimes in.

'You can get a style done really cheaply – someone comes in!' Brhe adds.

'I might go all the way,' Lillian says proudly.

'You might as well,' Ingrid says.

James walks into the lunchroom and Ingrid asks, 'Just back from a ciggie break, Ecuador?'

'Yes. Why?'

'No reason.'

'Anyway,' he says, 'this is your first and final Gail Warning. You're wanted back in the boardroom.'

■ ■ ■

'Most of you know Tyler from Sage & Scribner,' Gail introduces the guy at the front of the room. The next victim – and he has flown from Sydney for the privilege.

'Tyler – this is Ethan Grout, our new fiction buyer.'

'Hey.'

'Hey.'

Penny stands up to do her shtick. 'Tyler, before we start we thought we'd get to know you better with a quick quiz – just for fun.'

'Uh. Okay.'

'Favourite movie?'

'*Tremors 4.*'

'I don't know that one,' Penny concedes cheerily. 'Favourite M&M colour?'

Tyler looks about the room. 'Beige.'

Alejandra laughs. Brhe looks disoriented.

'It has to be an actual colour,' Ingrid protests.

'Your porn name?' Penny chuckles cheekily each time on this question.

'Lusty Borg,' Tyler replies.

'Your first pet was called Lusty!?' Ingrid is disgusted.

'Yes. She's dead.' That puts an end to that.

'Favourite author?' We are all expected by Penny to giggle on cue here, because of this question's relevance – what with this being the book industry and all.

'Dr. Phil.'

'From the *Dr. Phil* show?' Brhe asks.

'Ah, yes.'

'Finally, who would you turn for?'

'Heather Graham.'

The correct answer apparently, as provided by the previous two guys, is David Beckham. Ingrid and Brhe, beside each other, are beside themselves.

'Thank you, Penny,' Gail says.

I think that will be the last of the quizzes.

Tyler hands around a spreadsheet that is his attempt at completing a grid Gail had provided for all the reps. So far no rep has completed this to Gail's satisfaction.

'Tyler – you seem to have provided some of the figures but not all,' Gail says reproachfully.

'We just don't have the level of data you require, Gail. What I've done is given you a simple overview of sales by category by month – I'm sure this is more than enough to let you know how our business is trading.'

Alejandra sits up in her chair. Here we go again.

'Tyler – quite frankly I'm aghast. Aghast and speechless. You are the representative for your company and this is not, in any way, satisfactory. How can you possibly consider yourself a good account manager when you cannot provide rudimentary analysis? We look to you to do your job. We are the customer. This will need to be completed or we will not be able to support your titles. I'm totally speechless, Tyler. And aghast. Speechless.'

'Hardly speechless,' Alejandra mutters, just loud enough for me to hear, and I smile to myself.

Tyler, rather than looking admonished, appears bemused. This is most likely not the first time he's heard that speechless speech.

Gail has heard Alejandra mutter something and calls her out. 'Alejandra – are you not aghast?'

'I'm sorry?'

'Tyler's poor data – this makes all our lives difficult. Are you not, like me, aghast?'

I sense Alejandra struggling to subscribe to the terminology.

'*Aghast?* Me? Not so much.'

'So you feel happy with all this?' Gail makes a grand gesture that is meant to point out the spreadsheet but sweeps across the entire room.

'No, I am definitely disappointed,' Alejandra says.

'Good,' Gail says.

Gail makes a show of relenting to allow Tyler to present his books and eventually even succumbs to pulling out a 'Ker-ching' for the new James Patterson. Alejandra nudges me occasionally when something amuses her; Ingrid and Brhe do most of the amusing. Tyler is trying to remember the one-liners he's hearing – for tonight when no doubt all the reps get together for a laugh. Penny massages her list of five questions. Lillian wonders if she should really shave all her hair. The Hamster seems strangely quiet. Me – I'm wondering where the fuck I've landed.

10. Hump Day

'So ... another Heidi Klum.'

The stylist from Just Cuts, who has been sent in to raise money for leukemia, prepares to start on Brhe, while Ingrid, as Heidi Klum, returns to the lunch table, depositing a single gold coin into the collection basket that has even less value in it than the gift card I got from Auto World.

The temporary hair salon – one lady doing styles, while another shaves – has been set up at the end of the lunchroom where the entertainment centre is normally situated. Dale looks as though his very own living room has been invaded. His dark hair could do with a trim but he seems to have fashioned it into a post-shower faux-hawk at some point today – though when I arrived this morning I could have sworn it was more like bed hair – and he has passed on further messing about with it.

'What celebrity have you always wanted to look like?' I ask Alejandra.

'Sean Connery.'

'That'll help with losing some weight,' Ingrid says as she squeezes into the very centre of the table, the main function of which today is a viewing gallery to the salon.

Without Brhe to talk to Ingrid needs to decide whether to engage with what's available at the table. She looks as happy with this as if she'd paid for a seafood buffet and someone had already taken all the oysters. But soon enough her need to hear her own voice overrides her dissatisfaction with the audience available to her.

She complains about the progress of several reality shows she is pursuing, the cost of petrol, and the 'boringness' of the war in Afghanistan. Zooming in on less broader themes she, in hushed tones now, complains about her two-dollar haircut and the fact her sister does not have a television in her bedroom. Apparently she has been minding her vacationing sister's place because of a cat.

'How is Brhe going without you?' I ask so as to halt the list of things that irritate her from lengthening to irritating us.

'Can you believe she called me last night – even though she had nothing in particular to say?' Ingrid complains.

'Isn't that the point of friendship?' Alejandra asks, so sick of another salad that she's resorted to conversing with Ingrid.

Ingrid's attention is diverted by the mailroom guy arriving – waiting for a turn under the scissors. Deciding Alejandra is a lost cause, Ingrid leans over the basket of loose change and whispers at me, making me feel a little dirty given she seems to view me as some sort of confidante, whilst not taking her eyes off mailroom guy, 'He *just* pulled this bit of material out of his pocket, emptied his nose into it and put it *back* inside his pocket!'

'Handkerchief,' Alejandra says. 'That's called a handkerchief.'

We all silently agree that this particular group doesn't work.

I've decided that my hair really doesn't need to be any shorter: embarrassingly, my model stepbrother has sort of inspired me to give it a bit of a chance to grow. That said, I intend to place a note in the collection basket when nobody's watching. I'm not entirely sure if Alejandra intends to get her hair shaved – it would be a sad to hack away at those dark waves I reckon. Lillian is losing her own at the very moment and it's not looking so good.

Brhe's hair must not be as easy to convert into Heidi Klum and she is rapidly turning into Andrew G. For sure Ingrid notices this but says nothing.

Alejandra and I chat about the presentations from this morning and it feels like the first time in my three days here that we have had a lengthy interchange. And the first time I've really started to consider my role and contemplate my first buys – given my business card is going to say 'buyer'. If the Hamster ever gets round to sending them off for printing.

The virtually bald guy from the mailroom is called up by the stylist and Heidi Klum tells Andrew G that her hair looks great.

Lillian goes in search of a scarf.

Some young guy with soon to be gone brown locks gets up from the far end of the table and makes his way to take Lillian's place with the lady shaver. He stops to deposit a handful of coins in the basket and Brhe introduces me, 'Ethan, this is Dud Root.'

'Bud, is it?' I ask, putting out my hand.

'No, Dud!' Brhe says forcefully.

'It's Max, hey,' Max says.

'Hey.'

Brhe handled their break-up well.

Lillian returns with her skull being warmed by a turquoise scarf.

'Now you *really* look Algerian,' Ingrid says.

'Penny has hired someone for the third merchandisers' role,' Lillian informs Alejandra.

'Great,' Alejandra replies genuinely, making room for Lillian to sit between us – thereby saving her from getting caught in the Klum sandwich on the other side of the table.

'So, who is it?' Brhe asks.

'His name is Calesz apparently,' Lillian replies excitedly.

'Where's this one from?' Ingrid asks.

'Chechnya.'

'You gotta be kidding me!' Brhe cries.

'Is that even a place?' Ingrid, our nonfiction champion, asks.

'It's near Russia,' Lillian answers. Why she bothers I don't know.

'I guess it doesn't matter – all *they* do is fling Excel pivot tables about.'

'They' being merchandisers, not Chechnyans.

The mailroom guy's trim is over real quick and the stylist checks her list.

'Is Alex here?'

With no Wii to play, Alex, Sachin and Dale are nowhere to be seen.

'Ingrid, can you tell Alex it's his turn?' Alejandra asks Ingrid.

Ingrid looks to Brhe as if to say, *Which one is Alex?* To be fair, all these names are a bit confusing for me as well, so I don't want to be sent on this errand – but I've only been here for a few days.

'The Indian,' Brhe helps Ingrid.

'Oh yes, I know,' Ingrid smiles smugly at Alejandra. 'IT.'

'There are two Indian guys in IT,' Alejandra notes.

Ingrid looks as though she has fallen through the nexus of the universe where all things collide.

'How do you distinguish between them if you never bother with their real names?' Alejandra asks.

'One has a bonnet,' Ingrid tells her.

'Sachin's a Sikh.'

'I'll find him,' Lillian says and heads off.

Alejandra stands up and walks towards styling lady, as shaving lady makes Max, aka Dud Root, unrecognisable – probably his intention – and strikes up a conversation. I can't hear what they are saying but hope the stylist's suggesting her services to Alejandra rather than getting a Sean Connery from the shaver. They seem to agree to leave all as is, but I notice Alejandra slips her a note – orange at that. Alejandra comes back refreshed for more inane conversation – the diversion with the stylist was likely her equivalent of counting to ten.

Ingrid and Brhe are talking about *The Bachelorette,* which apparently is heading towards its climax. Not viewing it together last night means they have a lot to catch up on.

'Shut up! Darren is definitely going to win after last night!' Brhe tells Ingrid.

'I'm not sure about that – as they say, it's not over till the fat lady sings,' Ingrid says.

At that moment James enters the lunchroom. 'Fuck off, Ingrid. At least she's not brain dead.'

James thinks he is defending Alejandra. Alejandra squirms. Ingrid has no idea what she's said to incur this attack.

'What the fuck are you talking about, *Ecuador*?'

'Time for some fresh air?' Alejandra says to me and we get up quickly. She seems in no doubt that James will follow, as he does, and we head for the door.

Alejandra turns and says to the two table centerpieces, 'See ya Moe, see ya Werribee.'

■ ■ ■

Ever since Google reinvigorated the art of stalking it's become almost the fashion to have your very own ardent admirer – for those capable of allure, leastways. My sighting of that lady waiting outside Joy's house when I left the letter last week indicates Travis has one and it seems Alejandra does too. Isn't a stalker just someone who loves more than they are loved? Can't be that rare then.

I've already noticed that whenever Alejandra takes off for a ciggie, down to the loading bay, James, like the next tissue out of the box, always follows her. I'd thought it was to smoke – but as he struggles with his cigarette and coughs away I'm thinking this is still new to him. James pushes his garishly illustrated pack of ciggies at me and I reject the kind offer whilst trying not to appear like some sort of health freak.

Inspired by Ingrid, not something you'd imagine possible, we talk about nationalities and James says it's all a state of mind: if you can relate to a particular culture and feel at one with the people, then it doesn't matter if you share their blood. And vice versa.

'It's so random being born a particular nationality. Like you're meant to feel you belong to a club you never chose to join in the first place,' Alejandra muses, obviously enjoying her smoke, while James struggles with his

'Like being born into a particular family,' James notes.

'Or inheriting a bunch of colleagues you could never quite imagine existed,' I say.

Alejandra and James both smile.

'If I were to consider myself of another culture, I'd go something really exotic,' James says. 'Maybe Tahitian.'

'Nice food,' Alejandra jokes.

'So, Ethan, what are you anyway?' James asks.

'Nothing,' I reply.

'What do you feel like?'

'Albanian.'

A blond guy, wearing only jeans, a white singlet and several tattoos, wanders down to the ciggie spot. Alejandra and James seem to know him and introduce him as Guy – though they don't say what he does for our company, or even if he works with us.

Once the topic turns to the Hamster I realise he must work with us. He warns me that once she evades looking you in the eye you know you're a goner.

'I'll keep an eye out for that,' I say.

'Make sure you do, buddy,' Guy replies in a friendly tone.

Guy tells us about his greyhound that he trains every day. Apparently he will be Guy's escape out of working here – he just needs to get him winning some races. The dog sounds like he's Guy's best friend. Hopefully the rabbit at the track will become their third soon enough. I don't ask the greyhound's name just in case it's the same as one of Alejandra's siblings.

'Aren't you cold?' James asks Guy.

'I warm up – with all the hauling and stuff.'

Once Guy leaves I ask the others, 'What does he do?'

'No idea,' James replies.

'Smokes,' Alejandra adds.

'I wonder what time it is,' James says.

Though brisk, the sun is out and the blue has not been skimped on. The day is a nice one – outside that is.

'Nearly half past,' I say.

'Shit. I've got to issue the Gail Warning. You guys have to be back in the boardroom by half past,' James cries, and they stub their ciggies into the mini-sandpit and we head back to our work family's loving embrace.

11. The Joy of Lunchtime

Waiting for everyone to arrive for another day of frivolity, I sit in the boardroom ready to find out exactly what 'marketing' is – having previously presumed it was the roommate of numerology and the occult.

I've brought my mobile to work for the first time – not in anticipation of a noise from it, but because the lack of windows in the rooms these meetings gravitate to is killing my sense of time progressing – and set it in front of me.

Like a robot I'm sitting in the same chair I've held down for the last two days, and by doing so hope the established seating plan does not alter significantly with the inclusion of the marketing team and the new merchandiser, Calesz of Chechnya. I wonder what Ingrid is gonna call this guy as she's just as likely incapable of remembering his homeland as his real name.

Alejandra arrives and – I'd like to say it was the pull of my magnetism, but it was more likely due to the anti-charismatic force from the opposite side being so repelling – takes her previous spot as well – on my side of this long table.

As a forward thinker, Alejandra has turned up on a Thursday in Casual Friday clothes – dark jeans and matching long-sleeved

T-shirt. Ingrid, Brhe and I are more uncomfortably attired, as is the clearly stated preference of management.

Lillian arrives – her headscarf today is orange – not a single length of hair can be seen pushing its way out of darkness – and on seeing we are sticking to the same seating plan joins me and Alejandra. Penny arrives with Calesz, whom she introduces to us all, telling me I'm no longer the new guy, and balances the table by plunking him with Ingrid and Brhe.

'It's great to mix the teams up,' Penny says and heads to the far end of the table. Gail joins her, and then the Hamster arrives. I check to see if she looks me in the eye as she passes, but in fact her little face is so far into some report that her whiskers must be bending like so many pole vaults.

Finally, with a flourish, the star team arrives and takes the other head of the table – where, for the last two days, the reps from all the major publishers did their squirming and smirking.

Prince Mitch of the Principality of Marketing is escorted by Dale, who looks a little subdued without his Wii arm jerking out of control. From what I can ascertain Mitch is being fast-tracked through the company – he's probably my age, and already a manager. The cynic would suggest it's due more to his polished good looks and aura of success than actual talent or achievements, but I've not been here as long as the cynic.

'The Zac Efron of The Book Place,' Alejandra suggests to me as Mitch stands to commence his address.

'This is a place of extremes,' I whisper back to her.

'Most anything of value resides between extremes,' Alejandra notes, 'in the centre.'

'Like with Chicken Kiev?' I ask.

'Like with Chicken Kiev.'

The merchandisers all have their laptops with them as they are meant to pull out any data required at an instant. Mitch surveys team merchandise: Alejandra, Lillian and Calesz.

'Alejandra – could you keep the minutes.'

Apparently minute-keeping is too demeaning for his team, well, Dale, or the otherwise-engaged Hamster.

'Sure, I'll count the minutes.' Alejandra says perkily.

Mitch smiles enough to show he's not entirely humourless, but still has to reiterate, '*Keep* the minutes.'

Got it.

'Now, before we start with the agenda I think it is important to remind everybody about the dress code ...'

I make a point of not looking at Alejandra who seems to be tapping away faster than Mitch is talking. She could well be doing her emails.

'... which was reiterated by HR at this week's Monday meeting. The code is on the intranet and clearly establishes guidelines. No jeans. No collarless shirts. No running shoes. The complete list is there of what is, and is not, acceptable. Familiarise yourself with it.'

That said, Mitch continues, 'Now today: from the outset I want you all to take this opportunity to try and think outside the square! *My challenge to you* is wow us with your fresh and original plans! Don't be held back by what we always do! My motto is: *There is no such thing as a bad idea!*'

Mitch shares his motto with Osama bin Laden.

'Dale is going to present the results we received from the agency we hired recently to investigate our place in the Australian book market.'

Dale gets up and already looks ill at ease with what he has to endorse. Like Beckham Ang was with the dress code and punctuality rant the other day.

Mostly the agency's finding is stuff about the size of the industry, how we are number two behind Books Etcetera, and how, as determined by their research, we are seen by the market. After running through the agency's assessment of who our customer is, Dale wraps with the alarming news that our customer is Sigrid Thornton.

'The actress and fish-oil endorser?' Alejandra quits tapping for a second.

'I like her,' Brhe says.

'Yes, our core customer profile is a professional woman from the baby boomer generation. She has strong interests in our well-performing categories of health and diet. And is keenly interested in literature and the finer things,' Mitch tells us.

Alejandra starts to quake and tries to lower her head further toward the keyboard but is still visibly shaking.

'Why are you giggling?' Mitch asks her.

'It just looks funnier written down. Ignore me.'

'Does Sigrid read biographies?' Ingrid asks aloud, concerned about who's going to buy Stalin, Castro and Princess Mary.

'Should we call her?' Alejandra asks.

'Let's not get hung up on specifics,' says Mitch who has *specifically* narrowed our customer base to the character portrayed by that actress from *SeaChange*.

'Let's move on, thanks Dale' Mitch continues, 'Okay – let's throw about ideas on store layout for the peak lead-up period to Christmas. Anyone?'

'I propose that we create a real feeling of crowded stores and massive piles of books that are selling like hotcakes,' Gail suggests.

'That's where we want to get – *how* do we get there is the question?' Mitch tries to encourage us to really dig.

'Horse and cart,' Gail replies.

'Sigrid likes horses; back in the day she was in *The Man From Snowy River.*' Alejandra assures Ingrid across the table.

'I mean,' Gail starts to explain, 'if we create stores that feel like they are busy and heaving with great buys being snapped up, then it will be a self-fulfilling prophecy.'

'Okay,' Mitch concedes, 'how do we create that vibe?'

'With all the big titles – where we have lots of copies in all stores – we should planogram them so store staff know to stack them on the floor – great big piles on the floor.'

'Got that, Alejandra?' Mitch asks.

'*¿Porqué no?*' Alejandra says, tap, and tap.

'*My build on that* is we should also have loads of posters and hanging pieces – whatever we can get from the publishers – throughout the store to give that sense of *busy*,' Mitch says. 'And where is the *call to action* for the customer?' he asks the group.

'Maybe we can print redeemable discount vouchers in our Christmas catalogue – that will bring people into *our* stores rather than a competitor's store, given we normally have the exact same books,' Penny says, showing her new protégé Calesz that she is a manager too.

'No bad ideas!' Mitch chants, which I think is code to Alejandra to not bother recording that one.

'Next – promotions. What are some categories or series we want to focus on in-store in the months leading up to the holiday season?' Mitch asks.

'Hannah Montana …' Brhe announces.

'Ker-ching!' Gail calls out.

'… is going to be huge with the next movie and more tie-in titles coming out. They'll fly off the shelves!' Brhe declares triumphantly.

'We've decided to put the big books in piles, remember,' Gail reminds Brhe.

'They'll fly off the floor,' Alejandra says.

'What else? Something from fiction?' Mitch throws the hot potato of attention my way.

'As I'm still a bit green.' I'm holding on to new guy status a bit longer , Calesz the usurper or no. 'Any guidance is appreciated.'

'We haven't targeted science fiction for years,' Alejandra comes to my rescue.

'Anything meatier?' the well-earthed Mitch asks.

'What does Sigrid like?' Alejandra asks.

'Probably legal thrillers,' Ingrid replies.

'Huh?' Mitch says.

'She was a magistrate – in *SeaChange*,' Ingrid reminds us.

'Adult fiction's not that easy to theme by itself,' Mitch interrupts Ingrid's ramblings. 'What about a broad theme that can encompass literature, history, food, travel?'

'South America. All things Latin,' Penny suggests.

'On the right track,' Mitch says encouragingly.

'Or Africa?' Gail tries to steal it from Penny.

'I don't think so,' Mitch replies.

'Ker-plunk!' Alejandra says.

'Perhaps – if we are going with a geographical theme – we should look to Asia. More relevant, especially for travel and food. And a great history,' Mitch says.

'China,' Ingrid says.

That's it. *China*.

'What about it?' Mitch asks.

'Well. It's been around a long time.'

'Gringo,' Penny mumbles and Alejandra laughs, and taps some more.

'Maybe we'll take a quick lunch break and nut it out further after we've eaten,' Mitch determines, and just as people are starting to leave my mobile makes a funny noise. I look at it.

'It's called a text,' Alejandra tells me.

■ ■ ■

'Huh.'

'What?' Alejandra asks.

'It's Joy.'

'Who's Joy?'

'My stepmother I guess.'

'You guess?'

'Well, she married my dad just before he died,' I say.

'When did your father die?' Alejandra asks me.

'A few weeks ago.'

'Oh. I'm sorry, Ethan.'

'Thanks.'

'So, what does your stepmother want?'

'She's in the café across the road apparently.'

I explain to Alejandra that I'd called Joy last night just to let her know I had indeed got the job my letter had referred to. Her machine didn't mention anything about her coming to visit me here though.

'I'd better go down,' I say.

'What me to come along?'

Alejandra really must be stranded in boredom.

'Yes,' I say a tad too exuberantly.

'James and Greyhound Guy will have to make do with each other for ciggie conversation,' Alejandra says with a smile.

I don't think James will bother smoking today.

I fill Alejandra in on Joy's cancer as our lift descends.

Joy has a table out front, catching as much warmth as this day will likely offer. The thing is, she's more radiant than you'd expect from someone so sick, and although it looks like all she is eating is a chocolate brownie, she is getting through it well enough.

'Life is short,' Joy says as we approach, catching her take the gentle but eager bite of a vampire.

After introducing Alejandra I go inside to order coffees. It's still necessary to nod to most of the customers as any of them may be colleagues I was introduced to on my first day. Dale passes by the front windows with what appears to be a laundry bag, while the Hamster is sitting inside, deep in conversation with someone who appears even more senior than Prince Mitch.

Upon ferrying the coffees back outside I find Joy and Alejandra deep in conversation – soon they'll be tighter than I am currently with either of them. I don't actually mind, though, as after Joy finishes telling Alejandra about her specialist's appointment nearby she asks a few questions I wouldn't mind knowing the answers to.

'So, you and Damien have been together since school then?' Joy asks Alejandra.

'Yes – wow that makes it sound such a long time.'

'Not if he's the right guy.'

'I guess not.'

Now that I'm settled back down, Joy sweeps conversation back my way.

'So, Ethan, how's it going with the new job?'

'I like it so far – though this week has been a bit of a mess with meetings, meeting a thousand people, and more meetings.'

'That's sort of standard actually,' Alejandra jokes.

'How long have you worked here?' Joy asks her.

'Too –' Alejandra starts to reply

'Years?' Joy asks.

'Nope – way worse than that – too long.'

Don't go just yet …

'I should have brought a camera – it'd be great to have a photo of Ethan to show my friends,' Joy muses.

She talks about me to her friends? I thought I was destined to be a radar blip.

'Well, anyway, I thought I'd come say hi since I was nearby. Thanks for your letter and the phone message last night,' Joy tells me.

'That's okay. How's Travis? And Diego?'

'They're great, of course! Travis is walking like a champion and Diego is desperate to sleep with you again.'

'I'll explain that to you very shortly,' I say to Alejandra and Joy laughs. She seems happier than anyone I know.

12. Call to Action

Alejandra has smoothly segued from yesterday's attempt to introduce Casual Thursday to today's Cocktail Friday and is definitely the killer statement of her pod this morning. Lillian is still bald for leukemia and no one told newbie Calesz it was dress code posh today.

'You look nice, Mexico,' Ingrid concedes.

Which is sweet, but then, 'You *really* are a big fan of black.'

'I bet Damien noticed you this morning,' Brhe says.

'Well, he didn't think breakfast made itself,' Alejandra replies.

I'm wearing my wedding, funeral and interview suit. This is its fourth outing already. When I bought it a few months back I'd never have imagined it would have needed to visit a drycleaners so soon.

Ingrid and Brhe are keeping us in suspense – apparently they are not going to take the bus the company has hired to ferry us to the 'surprise' but are going home first to dress, hair and makeup themselves. Seems they know the location from an insider and want to make a grand entrance.

Beyond our pods the rest of the office is looking very slick indeed, except Dale who appears to have forgotten. He wanders past us meekly, seemingly on his way to the server room. From where I'm standing – by Alejandra's desk – I can see Dale enter a code in the door's keypad – his fingers trace the pattern: 1469 – and before going in, he looks around as if he's Superman entering a phone box. Maybe Dale is planting a virus that will wreak havoc so our 'special' day gets cancelled. Meanwhile, Alex and Sachin are down the other end of the floor, in conference with the Hamster who seems to be giving them grief over something.

'Cool suit,' Alejandra says to me.

'Thanks – who knew three months ago I'd have use for one at all.'

'Poor Calesz – we forgot to tell him. It's even worse because he's taken Casual Friday *very* literally.'

Calesz is dressed for a brawl. He has ripped jeans, armless AFL jumper and getaway trainers on. The army-style hair isn't doing the ensemble any favours either. Apparently he supports the Global Financial Crisis. Or maybe that's the Geelong Football Club. Me – not a big sports fan. They're just *other* people's teams.

'My second day – this is great!' Calesz leans in to our conversation; he appears visibly distressed.

'Don't worry – it's good to stand out occasionally,' Alejandra tries to reassure him, though he doesn't seem convinced.

Dale walks back past and he's dressed entirely differently to ten minutes ago. He *is* Superman. No one else seems to notice though. I head over to Dale's giant phone box and punch in the code.

The chill of the server room hits as soon as I close the heavy door behind me. It's like being in a giant freezer. In the middle of the room, where the pig and cow carcasses should hang, there is a bank of computers, while Alex and Sachin's workspace, the gutting bench, runs along the side of the room from the entry point. Alex seems to have left his computer midway through Skyping the Punjab. I wander around behind the computers and here it is: a fully stocked clothes rack, loads of boxes, a mirror, a pile of shoes, even a hook with a towel hanging from it.

'Have you seen Dale?' I ask Alejandra, after emerging from what appears to be Dale's apartment.

'No. Where did you go just now?'

'Just snooping,' I reply and head out, towards reception.

'James, have you seen Dale?'

'He's in the print station with Max.'

'Hey Max.'

'Hey.'

He seems to be glad I don't call him Dud Root, which is understandable.

'Dale, can I ask you a question?'

Dale is waiting for the colour printer to warm up.

'Sure.'

'Would you mind lending some clothes to Calesz?'

Dale looks at me. The jig is up. The printer starts giving it up as well.

'I guess not. Is he my size?'

'I reckon so.'

'Do you need the code?'

'Nope – got it. Thanks heaps, buddy.'

I wander off, leaving Dale silently watching his party invites print.

■ ■ ■

We assemble outside the front of the building to wait for our bus. The Hamster is checking everybody is here but even she struggles to be heard amongst the excited buzz and it's impossible to see her in the crowd. I'm hanging by Alejandra, hoping we'll get to sit together, but I doubt James will allow that.

A small, hotted-up white car with wide wheels and a determination to be heard, screeches out of the side lane and stops briefly where the bus is meant to be. Through the tinted glass I can see Ingrid; Brhe must be driving this thing. Brhe blasts her horn and is off again. Her numberplate is 'UUP4IT' – no question mark of course

– Brhe spends her entire punctuation allowance on exclamation points. She doesn't even slow down for commas.

'Now, now *I am* aghast,' Alejandra says.

As it transpires our bus has broken down so the replacement one takes an eternity to arrive. While waiting our team seems to bond like superglue in the absence of our two prime irritants. In the battle of boarding I eventually lose to a more determined James, but sitting next to Lillian is fine enough.

The bus finds its way to Albert Park and the consensus in the group is we are going to a day of watching polo. Everybody clambers out after the bus stops at the entrance to the ground. The Hamster has the ticket that covers all of us, so she holds it aloft and we have to try to follow her. We find Ingrid and Brhe, chuffed to have beaten us here, waiting out front. Both are dressed in less material than Arnie was given to utter in the *Terminator* script. They must be a tad chilly. To top it off, their Heidi Klum hairstyles have been jizzed to frenzy like Cameron Diaz's in *There's Something About Mary*.

'Hello ladies. How's business today?' Alejandra says to them as we pass through the entrance and follow the Hamster, who as Pied Piper has flipped *us* to being the rodents, to our marquee.

It is indeed posh: the marquee is heated and the lunch is going to be catered. There is a bar at one end, with a champagne glass pyramid as centerpiece, and tables scattered throughout the rest of the massive tent. In front of the marquee those interested in actually watching the polo gather. From what I can ascertain, the teams are all sponsored by elite companies.

'Wow, which corporation should we support?' Alejandra says as we claim a table nearest the heat with James, Lillian and a well-dressed Calesz.

'Hey, it's the League of Nations,' Ingrid says as she and Brhe walk by, stilettos sinking into the grass, on their way to a table more centrally located.

Sometimes I'm amazed at the terms that Ingrid *does* know.

'Mexico, Ecuador, Algeria, Russia and Evan,' Brhe runs through the list.

'Chechnya,' Calesz says.

'Ethan,' I say.

Me and Calesz head to the bar and get beers and wine, while Alejandra enjoys her ciggie and James coughs through his.

Around our table we take turns to find out more about one another, and though we mostly have nothing in common we have this – time and place. I don't attempt to make my life sound much more than it is and this audience seems okay with that. The bonhomie is so overwhelming that we even exchange mobile numbers – my phone won't know what's going on.

I notice Gail head over to Ingrid's table and tell them something that is apparently very exciting. Ingrid and Brhe leap out of their seats and pass us on their way to the bar.

'Apparently they're serving Pink Salamanders!' Ingrid announces.

'They'll probably serve you too then,' Alejandra says.

Brhe doesn't join Ingrid at the bar but hovers by us. 'I don't drink,' she explains.

'That's weird.' Alejandra replies. 'You often appear drunk.'

'I don't need to,' Brhe says. 'I'm just up!'

'Up 4 it,' Alejandra recalls the numberplate.

Ingrid returns by our table with her Pink Salamander just as we are being served plates of chicken and couscous salad. The waitress has managed to carry our five plates at once and squeezes between Ingrid and Brhe to deposit them in front of each of us.

'This looks pretty nice actually,' I say. 'I love chicken.'

'The salad is surprisingly good,' Alejandra notes.

'Did you see her hair?' Ingrid says, referring to the waitress and ignoring the food. 'What was that about?'

Calesz, proudly showing off his new outfit, continues to fetch beer and more beer and I find myself enjoying polo much more than I'd ever thought possible. I'm yet to see a horse though.

Lillian leaves us at one point and her seat, next to Alejandra, becomes a drop-in point for various people wandering from the bar to the viewing area. Penny stops by, Dale checks in on his clothes, and even Gail takes a turn. If I'm not mistaken, this crowd is turning into the downstairs crew at Baxter's. When Prince Mitch sits down we are all taken aback – what do you say to corporate royalty? But he's drunk enough to be less perfection and therefore less irritating. Ingrid turns up suddenly, and I realise that she is shadowing Mitch. They could easily be king and queen of this prom. Ingrid has acquired the role of official photographer and nudges between me and Calesz, purportedly to take a photo of Mitch, Alejandra and James.

Ingrid's lens zooms in and Alejandra sneers on cue.

After snapping, Ingrid takes a look at the shot and announces, 'Perfect!'

Alejandra leans over to me and says, 'She couldn't even be bothered to crop me and James out later.'

Originally I thought today would be like an Oscars ceremony – where only about one in five attendees leave with happy memories – but maybe they just don't drink enough at those events.

After a quick vomit in my mouth, I take another chug of beer, lean over the table and admit to Alejandra, whilst nodding in Brhe's direction, 'She sort of rings my bell.'

'Ding. Dong,' Alejandra replies.

We laugh about my lowering standards but all the while I avoid telling Alejandra it's been a while.

Then out of the dwindling blue: 'That was nice of you to get Calesz a better get-up. However you managed it.'

'It was easier than you'd think.'

'But, you did think – so anyway – it was cool.'

'Thanks, I –'

'Oh, my phone – that'll be Damien out front. See you on Monday, Ethan. Thanks for not being *them*,' she gestures towards some of the even less impressive members of our polo-viewing set, and is gone.

Soon enough the sun has found the horizon and Mitch has found Ingrid. Everybody's stories get funnier, even mine – if Brhe is any reliable gauge – and before long the few remaining people become the hottest and most hilarious group I've worked with.

■ ■ ■

I sense the sunlight's claim has now extended to the top half of my bed but I continue to keep my eyes closed. That is until I realise this sun is beating down not on me alone. Whoever it is next to me is now sitting up and preparing to leave.

'I'm going to go, Evan,' Brhe says.

I've slept with a misspelt soft cheese and she a mislabelled me.

'Oh. Okay. See ya.' Like a true gentleman I at least sit up as she closes the door behind her.

Fuck. Am I going to be Dud Root 2?

13. The Preserved Lemon

Brhe and I had shared something. Something I couldn't begin to describe.

Not until Sunday, yesterday, had I even thought to look at my mobile; seeing a text from Alejandra made me soar.

Don't get converted over to the dark side ☺ *Alejandra X*

It had been sent just after she'd left the polo. By the time I discovered the text it was too late to reply without lying, so it remains unanswered.

I get out of the lift and go through reception. James says 'Hey' without any weird inflection so I'm feeling a bit better. No doubt Brhe wants to keep this tryst as silent as me, and as Dud Root 1 would've liked his to have been.

Neither Brhe nor Ingrid look up as I approach our pod, so I sit down, turn on my computer and, casually as I can, glance in Alejandra's direction.

Alejandra taps her wrist so as to mock my tardiness and I'm well pleased that's the only retribution she has for me.

'How did you feel on Saturday?' she asks after leaning my way.

'Ah, you know, a bit hungover.'

'Just a bit?'

'A lot,' I reply.

All the while I'm trying to listen in on Brhe's conversation with Ingrid. This skill is beyond me – how do women do it?

Maybe this is it – maybe there'll be nothing more about it. I mean, I can't remember beyond the odd glimpses of time. Only catch is Brhe was sober – that's gotta make for some real regrets.

I have two emails – one from Bang – apparently Beckham Ang has decided today's morning meeting will be after lunch. The second is from Bcurtis. Please may Brhe's last name not be Curtis. Brhe's last name *is* Curtis.

It happened. Let's move on. Brhe.

Move on where? What direction?

She's barely a metre away from me, I can hear her clearly now – we should talk, that would be the adult thing to do. I decide to write back.

How was it?

I can't believe I sent that.

Safe.

Serves me right. Could she just give me the title of DR2 now and be done with it?

'I was *so* pissed I would have pashed Saddam Hussein's cadaver. Luckily I didn't have to.'

That came from the direction of Ingrid's glossed lips. From the sound of my pod-partners' conversation I'm assuming that Ingrid did get herself Mitched on Friday night.

'They don't call you Pashahontas for nothing,' Brhe tells Ingrid.

They call her Pashahontas? *They* really are stupid.

I decide to be a man. Oh, and Alejandra's suddenly away from her desk briefly so the coast is clear.

Standing up, I lean over my work-station partition and look at Brhe and Ingrid.

Their expressions back at me are as well glazed as Krispy Kreme originals.

'Thanks for your emails, Brhe –'

'You were *fine*,' Brhe interrupts me.

'I just want to check that we –'

'We're fine. You were fine. It's fine.'

Things are fine apparently. I sit down.

This is my first full day at my desk and so I have to quit worrying about Brhe taking the piss out of me and whether Alejandra knows, or would care. I start wading through all the stuff from last week. It's time to work.

■ ■ ■

The lunchroom is abuzz. Why is the morning meeting in the afternoon? Who hooked up with whom after the polo? Tickets for Pink's tour are on sale tomorrow!

I have to admit Brhe seems to have kept it pretty much to herself and her Siamese-colleague. It makes me envious in a way – it'd be nice to have someone to actually share this with. Other than Alejandra – she'd mock me mercilessly.

The Hamster deposits a couple of catering trays into the centre of the table, with leftovers from some high-powered meeting – lots of fruit, creepy sodden sandwich quarters and scraps of cheese.

'Who's gotten into the brie?' Ingrid asks, chuckling to herself.

Brhe chokes on a wedge of honeydew.

I look into space. Alejandra seems oblivious. It can't always be about me.

'How are the sandwiches?' Lillian asks, taking her place at the table.

Brhe holds up a mush of beetroot-sodden bread. 'Fine,' she says and flings it back onto the tray.

I'm not sure I like her use of the word 'fine'.

Beckham Ang comes into the lunchroom and has a girl with him.

'Hey, everybody, this is my wife, Fiona.'

'Here we go,' Alejandra says to me. 'One, two, three …'

Brhe leans over to Ingrid, 'Fang!'

'And there you have it,' Alejandra says. 'Time for fresh air.' And she's gone.

'What do you do, Fiona?' Lillian asks.

Fiona Ang looks at Beckham Ang as if to say, *Should I answer this?*

It must be harmless, so she admits, 'I'm in HR as well.'

'That's nice – both of you in the same profession. You can help each other out,' Lillian says kindly, though *profession* sounds like a strong word.

Beckham Ang decides to shuffle Fiona Ang away and Ingrid, thinking about the email database that gives us Bang and Fang, tells me, '*Ethan*, you should have seen us trying to find you on the email this morning. Why did you say your name is Evan?'

'I can't imagine I would have said my name is Evan.'

'Well, as it happens, there's no Evan in the company,' Brhe says.

'How did you solve this dilemma?' I ask.

'Brhe was swearing at the database saying, "Why won't Evan's name come up?" and your Mexican friend says, "Because it's Ethan",' Ingrid explains.

'Huh,' I say, but I'm thinking *Huh* for something entirely different – Alejandra's got to know that something happened with me and Brhe and she's not given me grief about it. That's good – I hope. It doesn't bother me for a second that even afterwards Brhe didn't know my name – I can hardly get to grips with her jumble of disoriented letters – but Alejandra has given me a free pass and that makes it all worthwhile somehow.

When Alejandra returns after her ciggie break I decide to quit stuffing around and give her the look that says *I know you know*, and she flings back a *Phew – now I know you know I know*. Who needs words?

'How old do you think Ethan is?' Brhe asks Alejandra, and finally I realise that she is enjoying prodding her about me for some reason.

'I *am* here you know,' I say.

'Forty-three,' Alejandra replies.

I laugh.

'Why are you laughing?' Ingrid asks me with a straight face.

'She's joking.' I explain.

'She's not smiling,' Ingrid says.

'Ethan is twenty-seven!' Brhe exclaims, preparing for a follow-up exclamation point. 'I assumed he was much younger!' There it is.

'Thanks,' I say.

It's a compliment in her world – but there's a slight sting of an insult in there.

'It's like he's preserved or something!' Brhe is running with the theme now.

'Like Dorian Gray?' Alejandra says, knowing full well they'll assume that's some guy in the operations department.

'Like a lemon,' Ingrid says. She's been watching *Top Chef*.

Shit, Dud Root is taken, I'm gonna be Lemon.

■ ■ ■

Lined around the wall, waiting to find out who is celebrating ten years service by not coming into work, I turn to Alejandra and finally call trade a spade.

'Do you think Brhe came home with me because I was the only white bread she could find?'

'Do you care?'

'I guess not.'

'Her diet may be very mainstream – doesn't mean you are.'

'Cheers!'

'Don't get too excited, Ethan – she considers spring rolls exotic.'

'Still, she's had one occasionally I assume?'

'Okay, you're a spring roll, satisfied?'

'With soy?'

'Mushroom-infused soy.'

'That's very kind.'

'You're welcome,' and she laughs.

Beckham Ang's manager stands at the front of the still unnamed large meeting room. Next to him are Beckham Ang and the Hamster. She's looking down at the floor – this can't be good.

'I need to make an announcement. Please listen carefully – we can have questions at the end.'

People start muttering but Beckham Ang's manager quells any murmurings with his raised hand.

'I've been asked to inform you, on behalf of the board ...'

'I thought *we* were the bored,' Alejandra murmurs despite the hand of quell.

'... that The Book Place has been purchased, overnight, by Books Etcetera.'

We are going to be Etcetera's Etcetera. Everybody turns to their significant others to exchange looks of horror. Alejandra seems oddly relaxed, so I turn to Lillian and Calesz. They are both too stunned to speak. Man, it's just Calesz's third day, whereas at least I'm a veteran at six.

'What does this mean for us?' a voice calls from the back of the Titanic.

'Questions at the end,' the Hamster reminds us. She's now freed up to look folk in the eye.

'We have had to maintain business as usual while negotiations continued over the last few weeks. Rest assured the final decision was only arrived at first thing this morning.'

'I'll be resting assured,' Alejandra says to me.

'I can't believe they had us doing all that stupid bonding ...'

'You enjoyed the bonding,' Alejandra says with a smile.

'… and those presentations. What was that about?' I moan like someone with years of time-wasting fast amounting to zilch.

'During the rest of the week each employee will be given the opportunity to reapply for their position in writing, and those who pass this stage will meet with the relevant manager from Books Etcetera.'

'What are the chances of us keeping our jobs?' somebody calls out, and the panel up front must now believe we *are* at the end as they quit trying to delay questions.

'It will be a case-by-case situation. There are many variables – including whether Books Etcetera requires someone with your particular skill set to complement their existing team.'

Calesz and I may as well start walking now.

'So we are stuffed!' a voice in the wilderness cries.

Already standard business terminology has been given the shaft.

'That's a bit defeatist,' says Beckham Ang's manager – or *is he* any more? 'Let's all take this a step at a time – each person's current manager will walk them through the application process and we'll take it from there.'

I can't believe I gotta get into that suit again – I might as well sleep in it.

14. Independence Day

While my reapplication for fiction buyer didn't progress past a written plea, it seems those who had to compete against their Books Etcetera doppelgänger, via a face-to-face interview with their prospective new manager, fared no better.

Word is that the only people to get rehousing are Mitch – the office hunk from marketing – and, of course, the Hamster survives like a cockroach. Even Dale, whose hourly rate for being in this place must equate to less than three bucks, has been considered poor value. I wonder where's he going to live. The rest of us are now, officially and entirely, superfluous.

Ironically, between Monday's announcement and today the team has grown considerably. There have been around half-a-dozen farewell cakes each day – for those who rejected the opportunity to hang on till the end of the week. Alejandra avoided the cakes by subscribing with Joy to the credo 'Life is short' and being the first to pass on the sham of reapplication, then leaving almost immediately.

I texted Alejandra this morning to advise her the Hamster was allowing everybody remaining to leave at lunchtime. One minute and seventeen seconds later she replied that she'd meet me out front and we could hang together. I've never felt so well hung.

'See ya buddy,' I say to Calesz as he leaves via the reception area where most of us have gathered to watch each other finally get set adrift, like Leonardo DiCaprio amidst the chunks of ice.

'What are you going to do for work now, Ethan?' Calesz asks me, searching for ideas.

'Not sure. Seek I guess. Dot com dot a-u I mean.'

'Me too,' Calesz says.

Gail and Penny are both stationed in the lift foyer to give the final manager's salute and I feel sorry for them as they seem to carry the additional burden of seeing their own teams smashed into mere individuals. They'd been a big improvement on the goons at Auto World.

'What about you guys?' I ask Alex and Sachin.

'No idea,' Sachin replies.

'I've got my other job,' Alex says. 'I do security at a pub on weekends. That should keep me going.'

'Alex was smart,' Sachin tells us. 'You should always have more than one basket for your eggs. Innit?'

'Innit,' I agree.

■ ■ ■

In just one fortnight I'd met more new people, and tried to memorise and match even more names to them, than I had the prior hundred. Alejandra, Ingrid and Brhe, Calesz, Lillian, Gail and Penny, Prince Mitch and Homeless Dale, the Hamster aka Rachel, Alex and Sachin from IT, James on reception, Max aka Dud Root, Bang and Fang, Greyhound Guy …

Most of these will no doubt slide right out of my life like hitchhikers, but my father had built up quite a posse by his life's end – simply collecting ones and twos as he went from job to job, location to location. If I carry just one person with me from here, and then the next place, and the next, and resolve not to outstay the expiration period of the slew of fresh names at any new workplace, then …

I mean what's the chance of winning the lottery if I don't keep buying tickets in each draw?

■ ■ ■

After assuring the crumpled Gail I'll be okay I remark, 'So, I didn't get to solve any number patterns after all.'

She doesn't know what the fuck I'm referring to.

It's a beautiful day: sunshine, light breeze; for the first time I notice that out front of our building there are actually a few trees, circled by pink flowers; even the pigeons look fresh. Alejandra lights up a ciggie.

'So, how were the last few days?'

'They changed their minds – I'm just here to tell you to come back to work.'

'Yeah, like you'd be smiling if that were true.'

Yeah, I am smiling.

'So what are we going to do?' Alejandra asks.

'Now? Or for the rest of our lives?'

'Let's focus on today at this point,' Alejandra says.

'My place is nearby – do you want to see it?'

'*¿Porqué no?*'

In the laneway that runs alongside Baxter's, Alejandra spots a roadworks crew having a break and asks one of them if she can borrow a lollipop sign they use for traffic.

'What are we doing?' I ask nervously.

'Joy said last week that she wants a photo of you.'

'Okay, but the sign? What's with that?'

'Come on – so many questions.'

Alejandra has me pose with the sign, which is about my height and simply says *SLOW*, and takes a photo with her mobile.

'What's Joy's number?'

Once Alejandra has sent the image she passes me her phone. The accompanying message reads: *Hi Joy – here's a photo of Ethan with his girlfriend Brhe – feel free to crop her out – Alejandra* ☺

'Cheers.'

'No worries, mate,' Alejandra replies in the thickest accent she can manage.

The lights are on in Baxter's – there's always someone home.

'How do you like living in a pub?' Alejandra asks me as we step from the outside sunshine into the darkened but lively interior of the main bar.

'It's never lonely,' I reply.

'I guess not – you've always got him,' Alejandra says, nodding discreetly at a guy wearing a jacket fastened up those few too many centimetres. This look seems to magically deduct at least fifty IQ points. *Whereas* my style is best summed up by the fact that I have an article of clothing that goes by the name of 'my good T-shirt'.

'How come you don't enter through the side street?'

'It's nice to see everyone's home.'

'I'd rather come home to an empty house. Growing up with three brothers – give me some space.'

'What about now?' I ask. 'With Damien?'

This is the first time I've discussed the mysterious partner with Alejandra.

'I still like my independence,' she replies, before adding, 'at times.'

She's not giving much away.

'Did you bring Brhe through here?' Alejandra asks.

'Can't say that I recall.'

'That's lovely,' Alejandra says, smiling mock beatifically.

We make our way up the stairs, past my neighbours' doors and through mine.

'It's very small,' I say, so as to save Alejandra the trouble of avoiding the elephant in this spaceless room.

'I don't know. It's got a certain charm and everything you need,' she says kindly, then, 'and some you don't.'

Alejandra has spotted, it's sort of hard not to, the massive fish tank under the sole window.

'That's Mister Fantastic,' I tell her. 'He's got the amount of space *you'd* appreciate.'

'Even I reckon you could afford to *squeeze* a few more in, Ethan.'

'I started with more – over time they've just sort of drifted up.'

'Ethan – get him some friends.'

'I'll work on it,' I say.

Alejandra gazes out the window – it really only takes a few seconds before that becomes the only place to look.

'*MOVIE STAR IN SEX STORM*,' I read out today's news from the newsagent's sell sheet.

'A storm of sex – sounds hot!' Alejandra does a perfect imitation of Ingrid. Or Brhe. Same same.

'Why do celebrities step out, get caught in sex storms, create love nests, live in compounds, and surround themselves with entourages?' I ask.

'It's no different to our lives – they just have a better thesaurus.'

Alejandra's eye catches on something beautiful.

'Oh, yeah, that's my stepbrother Travis.'

'He's sure in your face,' Alejandra says.

'Yup.'

'Do you guys get along?'

'I barely know him. He seems friendly enough but I reckon we have nothing in common. I bet *he* has an entourage and is forever stepping out.'

'So, what should *we* do?'

'Do you want to watch a DVD?'

'Does it mean I have to sit on the bed that still remembers Brhe?'

'It's forgotten her.'

'That's okay then.'

'Have you seen *Borat*?'

'No.'

'Cool.'

I set up the DVD and we both sit with our backs against the wall, legs outstretched, and I crank up the volume to drown out downstairs and outside.

'Will your neighbours,' Alejandra taps on the wall above her head to remind me they live just centimetres away, 'mind the noise?'

'They won't be home, and anyways, I have to listen to them having sex often enough. *And* he's getting better so it's lasting longer.'

'You've got it all,' Alejandra tells me and pats me on the head.

I've seen *Borat* a bunch of times and it remains funny – even if it's as fake as reality television and we've since learned the Kazakhstan stuff was in fact filmed in Romania. You can be too precious with comedy.

As the credits roll I worry Alejandra'll just up and leave and there'll be a text or two over the next couple of weeks. That we won't have set enough glue to make a friendship stick.

'Okay then,' Alejandra says, scrambling off my bed.

Here we go – here she goes.

'I'm off to my parents' place tonight. Friday night is always too much family and too much food.'

'Damien too, I guess?'

'Yes.'

'Well – have fun,' I say.

'Do you want to come along?'

15. Meet the Garcias

'What should I bring?' I ask Alejandra.

'Whatever you like to eat and drink. Oh, and something to sit on.'

'Ah ...'

'We *don't* do BYO.'

'Oh, cool.'

'Let's walk to Flagstaff station – the fresh air will do us good and I can squeeze in a couple of ciggies,' Alejandra says and we head off, taking as many laneways as we can – bypassing the main thoroughfares as much as possible. Our route is a bit 'snakes and ladders' but there's no rush when you're without employ.

Crossing through a park Alejandra spots something at the base of a massive tree. It's a small bird being tended to by a larger one.

'Do you think it dropped out of its nest?' I ask.

'Maybe ...' Alejandra is distracted. Her ciggie hand is even empty.

'Should we try and move it back into the tree?'

'It looks okay ...'

Alejandra sits on the grass mesmerised, and I follow suit. We watch the bigger bird fuss over the younger one – who does seem fine. It might just be we caught them midway through a flying lesson.

'Is the bigger one the parent?'

'Let me ask them,' Alejandra says.

Both birds start hopping around on the patch of dirt that acts like a moat around the tree's trunk and then, something you'd only notice if you were looking, they are both suddenly airborne and above us in the tree's canopy somewhere.

'We'd never have seen that at The Book Place,' Alejandra tells me and we continue on our way.

'So, you're happy I take it?'

'I'm about five kilos from happy, I reckon,' Alejandra says.

To be finished working at our office I meant.

'What are you going to miss?' I ask her.

'Oh, I don't know – mandatory lunchtimes or living in a pod – it's hard to choose.'

'Are you going to miss me?'

Too much? Too soon?

'Where'd you go?' Alejandra asks.

■ ■ ■

'Did she just say *grouse?*' Alejandra whispers, looking at me with her subtle smile.

The train to Footscray is full of the types you'd expect to see headed there at this time of day. Off-peak people. Facing us are two girls reconnecting after apparently having run into each other for the first time since high school. One has a daughter not quite old enough for kindergarten.

'Have you got any kids?' the mother says to the other.

'No, thank fuck.'

The kid's eyes open wide.

'Hey – shut it,' Alejandra says, staring them down.

Both of the young women look at us as if we are shit on their ugg boots and carry on laughing about old times.

Heading out of Footscray station Alejandra points to the left and says, 'My family lives just over there.' And we go right.

Footscray Market is packed with Vietnamese stallholders selling every type of food imaginable and a vast array of plastic items to store it in. I follow Alejandra around like James, as she is greeted by familiar faces and selects seafood, meats, fruits and vegetables – enough for a family.

We buy fish that still has eyes, limes that come specifically from Tahiti, black beans that get measured out by the handful, and vegetables with flaws.

'Do you like okra?' Alejandra asks me after she's already paid for it.

'Yes, actually. I've tried it once but I can't say it's a staple.'

'It's not for us either – I tend to get bored with cooking one thing over and over so this is something new to the repertoire.'

Best not ask her if she's cooked number 52. I've had it a squillion times but doubt I could list most of the ingredients.

'How long has your family lived here?' I ask Alejandra as we schlep the food back across the railway overpass.

'We left Mexico City when I was ten and landed in Footscray.'

'So, where do you and Damien live?'

'Our apartment is only a few blocks from my parents' place. I've not gone far, huh?'

'Well, you have come all the way from Mexico.'

'I guess. Feels like I've slowed to a halt now though.'

'How long have you been with Damien?'

'We met around seventeen.'

At the apex of the crossover we stop to give our arms a break and take in the view. Below us the wide streets are lined with old wooden houses with cosy porches and backyards. The occasional modern apartment block has been plonked onto the grid and the entire game board is overshadowed by the skyline, which offers the long expanse of the Westgate Bridge, glimpses of the city, and giant mechanical apparatus – that look like the stars from *Transformers* – picking at container ships that languish in the wharves.

'I like a busy view,' I say appreciatively.

The family house of Garcia is just a short walk into the grid – meaning the home is of the older type and not as large as you'd expect for a family of six. We walk straight in and immediately I can hear lots of talking and laughing coming from the back of the place. Something is already cooking and I prepare myself for variances to my standard diet *and* for another fresh batch of names.

Alejandra drops her load of shopping, and I do the same, onto the table in the kitchen where three identical-looking young guys are sitting as if waiting for dinner to be served. Looking into a giant pot on the stove is an elegant, petite woman with greying hair in a bun. She turns around and offers a subtle smile I've seen before.

'Mum – this is Ethan.'

'Hello, Ethan – welcome to our home.'

'Thanks Mrs Garcia.'

'So, you work, I mean *worked*, with Alejandra.'

'Yes – for a short time.'

Turning to introduce her sons who are variously reading magazines and playing with their mobiles, Mrs Garcia tells me, 'Ethan – these are Alejandra's brothers – Apollo, Hugo and Diego.'

'Huey, Dewey and Louie,' Alejandra says at the same time.

'Hey, I'm confused enough.' I poke Alejandra in the ribs.

I shake hands with each of them and try to ascertain any distinguishing features: barely a centimetre separates them and I swear they've split two hundred kilos entirely evenly. Thankfully, unlike their sister, they don't all stick to black clothing and I'm pretty sure it's Apollo with the red hoodie. I wasn't quick enough with the other two though.

Sensing that I'm wondering why they're all home in the

afternoon, Alejandra tells me, sceptically, 'They are at university, apparently.'

'Hey, we've done our ten hours this week!' one of them protests and his womb-buddies laugh.

Alejandra checks on the pot her mother is tending and Mrs Garcia smiles at me warmly, so as to invite conversation.

'Wow, giving birth to triplets,' I say.

'Alejandra weighed close to the same as the three boys together,' Mrs Garcia tells me proudly. I'm not sure Alejandra is as fond of that anecdote.

'Still does,' Apollo calls out from the table.

Through the window I can see the modest-sized backyard with, as its centerpiece, a well-broken-in barbecue constructed of besa blocks. The well-tended lawn is ringed by fruit trees and vines, and behind the barbecue is an outdoor table made of warped wooden planks that hover over at least ten chairs – no two as identical as the lads at the indoor table.

An older guy who I imagine is Mr Garcia is shifting twigs and coals around under the barbecue's hotplate, though nothing is lit yet.

'So, what do you think of the soup?' Mrs Garcia asks Alejandra, who has tasted it, and dropped in shakes, grinds and squeezes of about five more ingredients.

'Nice, Mum. I'll let it simmer a while longer before adding the shellfish.'

Seems Alejandra has taken over from her mother and Mrs Garcia drifts into the compact living room that backs onto the kitchen and starts ironing a pile of jeans that nearly reaches the ceiling.

'No creases!' Hugo or Diego calls out.

'What time's dinner?' Diego or Hugo asks Alejandra.

'At least an hour.'

'Pub?' Apollo asks them both.

'Pub.'

'We'll be back for dinner,' one of them announces. 'Don't eat it all, Alejandra!'

'Ethan's stepmother has a dog called Diego,' Alejandra tells him.

Cool – Diego's the one with Converse trainers.

'Ruff,' Diego replies.

'The pub is just down the street,' Alejandra tells me. 'They'll be playing pool – you can join them if you want.'

'Nah – it's cool. I'll hang here.'

■ ■ ■

'That'll be Damien.'

Alejandra hands me the pliers and says, 'Keep plucking' – fine bones out of the raw fish fillets that is – and heads down the hallway to answer the door.

'Hi.'

'Hi.'

No kiss from what I can tell.

'The guys are at the pub,' Alejandra offers.

'What time is dinner?'

'About half an hour.'

'I'll tell them.'

And she returns.

'You haven't done much.'

'I'm no cook,' I say.

'No matter.'

'Can I help?' Mrs Garcia asks after somehow breaking the jeans into three separate crisp piles.

'I've put the meat for barbecuing on this platter – can you take it out to Dad?' Alejandra passes the serious slabs of meat to her mother, who takes it out to the old guy who quite possibly never comes inside.

■ ■ ■

'Is it too cold to eat outside?' Mr Garcia finally comes indoors, carrying with him the tray of cooked meat.

'I think so, Dad,' Alejandra says, kissing him on both cheeks. 'This is Ethan.'

'Hi Mr Garcia.'

'Hello young man. Are you a friend of the triplets?'

'No. Alejandra's.'

'Oh. That's nice.'

Alejandra sends her father out with a warm hug, fish adrift in marinade, and cooking directions, while Mrs Garcia starts setting up the kitchen table.

'Alejandra – if you and your father sit at either ends of the table we can comfortably fit three people each down both sides.'

'Okay.'

The triplets and Damien return from the pub and start to assemble around the kitchen table.

'Damien, this is Ethan,' Alejandra introduces us.

'Hey,' I say, shaking his hand.

'Hey.'

Damien wears a suit, though he has loosened the tie slightly so as to give his thick neck a chance to breathe. I had anticipated a Prince Mitch level of looks so am partway delighted.

'How's the world of high finance, Damien?' Mrs Garcia asks, somewhat formally given he's been with their daughter since last century.

'There's a crisis *still*,' Damien says crisply.

Mrs Garcia places me between herself and Damien on one side of the table, with the triplets on the other. The food lands on the table and it looks mostly unfamiliar but fantastic at the same time.

'Can you pass the oh-krah, Ef-an?' Mr Garcia asks me.

'Sure,' I say.

'Ok-*ra!*' Damien tells Mr Garcia.

I make for the tower of soft white tortillas but can't see any mince.

'You put a spoonful of black beans in first and then slices of barbecued fish, a splash of lime, and then top with guacamole and sour cream,' Alejandra tells me, preparing one for herself.

'I'll take the toppings, shall I,' Damien says pointedly to Alejandra, though from where I sit he carries much the same weight overall – his is just mostly positioned on his fat head.

'So, Ethan – have you got a new job lined up?' Mrs Garcia asks me.

'I'll have a look on the internet this weekend and blast off some applications,' I reply. 'So, not as lucky as Alejandra.'

'What's that?' Damien says.

'I told you,' Alejandra tells him, without extrapolating.

'She has an interview next week with a book publisher,' says the brother who, by process of elimination, must be Hugo.

'I know – Lane and Tate,' Damien says.

'Tate Lane,' Hugo says shortly.

'Well, don't go hungry in the meantime, Ethan – there is always dinner here if you need it.'

'Thanks Mrs Garcia.'

The triplets end up being good value and provide the entertainment for the rest of the meal. These photocopies, more than anyone, are able to pick up on each other's subtle, individual differences and mine them mercilessly.

After dinner I support Mrs Garcia's decision that the triplets have to clean up and say my farewells.

'So, thanks heaps for feeding me – I won't need to eat for a week,' I tell Alejandra as she sees me out.

'You're welcome.'

'We should catch up again soon,' I say.

'*¿Porqué no?*' she replies, which basically means yes I've ascertained.

'We will *Ef-an*,' Alejandra adds with a grin, and then, 'Thanks for not correcting Dad, by the way.'

'Oh. No worries.'

I walk back to Footscray station – in the distance I can see the giant transformers at the wharves – still now, but lit up. I beam back at them.

16. Home Alone

Instead of taking the train all the way back to the city I get off prematurely at North Melbourne station. I want the sensation of returning to a home that's full of family life; not just empty rooms lit up in pretence, or a crowd of swaying strangers who don't hang around beyond closing.

The main street is still buzzing with the end of the working week and my legs move quickly, trying to outrace my head. What will Joy and Travis make of me just turning up – with nothing particular to say?

My head beats me there and instead of pressing the buzzer I sit on the step more commonly reserved for Travis's groupies. They might not even be home just now, but either way it doesn't feel empty. Resting the back of my head on the brickwork beside their door I close my eyes momentarily. I hear Diego – the dog, that is – tapping his claws on the wooden floors, pacing up and down the hallway.

■ ■ ■

'Is your dad home Ethan?'

Was she just waiting for me to return from the corner store?

'Not at the moment Mrs Lopez.'

'Well, would you like to join us for dinner?'

'He's just gone to get takeaway.'

'I haven't seen his car in a while?'

'It's being repaired.'

I realise this makes no sense but slip in the front door before further interrogation, turning on the porch light to prepare for my father's supposedly imminent arrival.

The washing machine makes the tune that announces it's finally exhausted of spinning out of control, so I climb onto a stool and shift my uniform into the dryer above it. This should shut them all up for a bit.

Leaving the light on in the laundry – no need to exclude this room from my celebration of electricity – I return to the living room and my familiar progression through the collection of videos stacked by the television.

Every film my dad has worked on. Normally I sequence them in date order and tonight it has come back around to *Inspector Echidna*. He laughs about that one now.

The sound of a skateboard's tail scraping along our front path has me putting down my packet of chips and pausing the spiky hero.

'Ethan!' Karl calls out from the front door. He gave up ringing the bell a while back – due to his lack of success at gaining attention that way.

I open the door slightly. Even with daylight savings it's nearly dark outside.

'We're going down to the skate park,' Karl says, peering past me into the house.

'I can't,' I say.

'See ya in class tomorrow, then.'

'Okay.'

The phone rings. This'll be Dad, if it's not the school counsellor again. Deciding to risk it, of course, I once more stop the movie.

This time, if it's her, I'll say he's taking a shower.

'How you doing, buddy?'

'Good. How's Chicago?'

'Unbelievable! They're a great bunch,' Dad says. 'And guess what, Ethan – it's five in the morning here, and snowing!'

'Cool.'

'Have there been any calls I should know about?'

'Nope.'

'Have you had dinner?'

'Yes.'

'What did you eat?'

'Um. Fish fingers.'

'Okay. I'll call you again soon. I love you, buddy.'

'I love you too.'

The movie really does suck, apart from the cinematography, so I eventually fast forward to the best part – the credits – and then turn off enough lights to satisfy the neighbours. After checking underneath the beds and inside any cupboard large enough to house a bogeyman, I sign my report card, set the alarm and get into bed.

■ ■ ■

The sound of a car alarm starts me awake and I stretch my back against the brickwork. Its real cold now and I turn to see that Joy's place is in darkness. I get up and head back to *Bright Lights, Big City*.

17. Spring Chicken

It is the season to be jobless. Spring has not long arrived and isn't fucking about this year. Global warming is hot.

Today's plan was to walk from lunch to dinner. This I am just about to achieve, having found a new McDonald's in Yarraville – which not only allowed me a fresh location to order from a stale menu, but the opportunity to discover there really is a street in the suburb called Lois Lane, and then, on the way home, to casually case both Alejandra's former and current residences in Footscray, before Joy's place in North Melbourne, where I also chickened out. The only knocking was my knees – not just from trying to get up the guts to rap on a door and set about building something, but also having agreed this morning to accepting a position in a call centre.

The telephone interview was over within minutes and I soon realised that unless I'd rung up and replicated the sound of a fax machine the job was mine. Anyone's. The guy who interviewed me wrapped up the call by saying he *hoped* to see me tomorrow and around nine-thirty would be fine but don't worry if I'm running late. This is making me think I'd better get started on finding the next job before even commencing this one.

The twenty-four-hour internet café on Swanston isn't open.

'Ethan!'

My name is not so rare these days – I'm not going to make a goose of myself and imagine I'm *the* Ethan.

'Hey, Ethan, up here!'

I see Travis up on the side of a building, not as a billboard, but more alive. He's leaning over the balcony – two levels up – of what appears to be a happening bistro.

'Wait there, I'll come down.'

He's gone from the balcony but I see his friends looking down. Looking down and looking down at me. They're not what I'd call the Yarraville McDonald's set.

Travis is so enthusiastic, and also possibly dubious I'd hang around waiting, that he's run down the stairs, tripping on the last couple before reaching the street.

'Hey, buddy, what are you doing here?' Travis says, pushing out his hand, which he's dusted off.

'I actually live just down a bit,' I remind him, shaking his hand.

'Where've you been?'

Does he mean since weeks back when I'd returned his dog or today? Do he and Joy *expect* me to maintain communication?

'Just walking.' I take his query as being about today and leave out the bit where I wandered past their place without knocking. At least there was no woman sitting out front on Travis-watch this time.

'Where are you headed?'

Each of his questions sounds like I'm at some personal-growth seminar.

'Just on my way to get some dinner.'

'What are you having?'

'Fifty-two.'

'Huh?'

'Oh, it's a chicken thing.'

'Okay,' Travis says, then, 'Hey Ethan – I'm just upstairs with a few friends – come up and say hello.'

I'm trying to discount him as aloof and self-absorbed but he's really not making it easy.

'Thanks, Travis, but I don't think I can,' I reply, taking another look up to the balcony of beautiful people.

I feel myself turning a little crimson – not as bold as Travis's shirt, but enough that I need to change the focus off of me being pathetic. Travis has got all these great friends and I've not only missed the boat, I didn't even know there was a boat.

'How's your mum by the way?' I ask.

'She's sticking in there – pretty tired though, but still gets out of the house each day.'

'Say hello for me,' I say.

'I'm not letting you go so easy,' Travis says, before shaking my shoulder and adding, 'Just come up briefly – I'm sure the number 52 will wait.'

He makes it sound like a tram.

'You're with your friends …'

'Uh-huh. That's the point – I want you to meet.' Travis is persisting longer than I'd have thought he'd bother. 'You are family after all.'

I guess he does manage to sway people into paying three hundred dollars for jeans.

'*¿Porqué no?*' I say eventually.

■ ■ ■

'Everybody, this is my stepbrother Ethan,' Travis announces to the three people sitting at the intimate table on the balcony overlooking Swanston, before darting off to find an extra chair.

They continue their conversation – the older guy, with a plume of silver hair set against mahogany skin, who kindly allows me to fall into the sweep of his eyesight so I might feel included. The girl meanwhile has the dead expression of a Russian supermodel, but even as a corpse she is stunning. Hopefully any plans she may have to eat when she gets older will bring her back to life.

The other guy, about Travis's age, is similarly tall and lean but in contrast has dark features set against pale skin. He has the familiar horse-face of a gaunt male model and is arguably not as good-looking as Travis, though I sense, by his carriage, he wouldn't concede this for a second. Both he and the old guy seem Australian, though they have a slight case of non-specific-foreign-accent syndrome.

In the time it takes Travis to return I'm still none the wiser as to any of their names.

'So, let me introduce you.' Travis assumes correctly that this lot won't have offered up their labels to me of their own accord.

'This is Zac,' Travis says and the younger of the guys nods his horse-face in acknowledgment, 'and this is Tatiana, and –'

'The Silver Fox!' Zac jumps in. Travis laughs.

'– this is Siimon.'

'Two "i"s,' the older guy warns me.

'He likes to be called the Silver Fox,' Zac reiterates what is obviously a private joke. Travis laughs again.

'Either name is fine,' Siimon says proudly – the owner of two names *and* two 'i's.

On closer investigation I can see that Siimon has had work done on his face – some sort of Botox/plucked eyebrow combo – and looks to have a permanently quizzical expression. The Silver Fox is no spring chicken.

Tatiana has finished her champagne and calls over the waiter with all the energy she can muster.

'Ethan – what do you want to drink?' Travis asks me, handing over a menu. 'We're ready to order food too if you want dinner.'

'That's cool – maybe I'll just have a drink.'

I look at the drinks list, realise I've only enough money for the sort of dining I normally do, and order a Coke – the water is too expensive. Tatiana, unprepared to introduce food into her diet, sticks to champers while the three guys try to outsoup and outsalad each other – no one daring to look beyond the appetizers.

The girl who takes our order looks just as sophisticated as any of the clientele – that's when you know you're in a swanky place. She has a name badge that claims she goes by *Beverley*, but from what I understand these are notorious for being handed around amongst hospitality staff, with their massive turnover rates, like sweets. With name-switching as rampant as at the racetrack or in a fifties maternity ward, I assume she's too hip-looking to be a real Beverley. Unless, of course, her full name is actually Beverley Hills.

Travis checks his phone.

'Saul can't make it,' Travis says to himself.

'So, anyway, I do the casting, get a call-back, and they ask me – can they see my portfolio again? I mean, I'm right there in front of them, what's more to see!' Zac implores the others.

'Three fittings. Three in one day! I hate this job,' Tatiana says.

'Do you think – skin darker or lighter against my hair?' Siimon asks the table.

'I end up saying – book me, don't book me. Let my agent know what you want to do. Idiots huh?' Zac rallies on, even neighing a little.

'If they expect me to do hair and makeup three times as well, then forget it,' Tatiana says.

'You can't be the creative director and not have a look that doesn't catch the clients' eye as well as the models you find for them. So, darker or lighter? Or do I change the hair to match my skin tone better?' Siimon asks.

'My agent can sort it out – that's what their cut is for,' Zac says.

'One hair and makeup – that's it!' Tatiana decides.

'It's getting warmer,' Siimon says, peering skyward. 'Maybe my whole vibe should reflect this.'

Travis checks his phone.

'Alison probably can't make it,' Travis says to himself.

How many friends does Travis have exactly?

'I'm sorry, what was that?' I ask of Siimon's post-question expression.

'I didn't ask you anything.' Siimon looks at me like I'm a fool. A fool he's just asked a question.

Fuck – try to not look at him in the forehead again.

The food arrives – the waiter delights in announcing Zac's: 'Here we have the Greek salad *without* feta.'

As if to say, *The Greek salad less the Greek.*

I glance at Travis's soup – there is no decent place to set your eyes at this table – and he tells me, 'Borscht.'

Within seconds Travis has spilt some of the borscht, but given his shirt was already coloured beetroot it's no matter.

Zac looks over at Travis with a concerned expression and asks, 'Travis – are you worried that pulling your hair back behind your ears like that all the time might cause them to permanently stick out?'

'That hair is his trademark,' Siimon says quizzically, before adding, 'And struggling to walk.'

Zac and Tatiana both grin.

'I hadn't thought about it,' Travis replies, patting at his ears.

'Probably too late now,' Zac says.

Siimon offers about the chunky pieces of toasted baguette that came with his asparagus soup. Everybody declines of course.

'Wow, this is the stuff that proves Travis truly is as thick as toast,' Zac says, pointing at the baguette bits.

I amaze myself at how that makes me sting but Travis doesn't seem bothered at all, laughing at his mate's wit.

Soon enough Travis's friends are back into their barrage of out-loud thoughts and are as difficult to follow as the panel on *The View*.

'I might get going, Travis.'

'Oh. Okay. I hope it wasn't too much industry talk for you?'

'No – it's sort of interesting actually,' I say.

'Hey, why don't you come along to a magazine launch that I've got tickets for? Next Friday night.'

Are you fucking mad?

I look at Travis – he genuinely seems to want to include me in his life – and before the shutters have a chance to come down I find myself saying, 'Yeah – maybe. Okay.'

Am *I* fucking mad?

18. I, Pod

'Ivan here is the team coordinator and will mentor you during your time with us. Ask him anything!' says the old bloke who is delighted I've actually turned up, though he doesn't sound overly confident I'll be here long enough for cake.

'Cheers,' I tell him and he wanders back to his office to work on finding my replacement.

The vast open-floor area has around a hundred people, sitting in large pods that each hold five people – at least I'm moving up – and there is the distinct smell of a fish tank with aging water. These podsters all wear Britney-style headsets, and go in and out of conversations, talking simultaneously like a table of Travis's friends.

'You've made his day,' Ivan, built like a rugby player, says before shaking my arm loose.

'Yeah, it seems like it,' I reply.

'Go ahead, make my day,' Ivan says for no apparent reason.

'Huh?'

'Clint Eastwood,' Ivan says.

'Yep.'

'Have you worked in a call centre before?'

'No, but I'm sure that –'

'Don't worry – there's nothing to it. Just don't take it too seriously.'

I like the sound of that. I'm warming to Ivan now.

'Remember, *they* are out there and you are in here. They can't strangle you even if they want to.'

As Ivan leads me towards a pod with two empty spaces he turns back and whispers, 'I see dead people.'

'This is Mason, Shearer and Weaver.' Ivan introduces me to a woman and two men but none of them is free to talk.

'Last names?'

'Yes – it's a policy here – only team coordinators are known by first names. Sort of reverse snobbery. It's a policy.'

If their family names are any indication, they all come from a lineage of workers.

'So I'm ...'

'Grout,' Ivan tells me flatly.

We both sit down in Ivan's segment of the pod so he can talk me through the role.

'Though,' Ivan says, pointing in the direction of each of our teammates in turn, 'I prefer to call them Wanna, Gonna, and Coulda. Wanna travel overseas, Gonna become a fireman, Coulda gone to university.'

'Maybe I'll stick with their surnames,' I reply, as Ivan starts flicking through his newspaper like an Arab – from back to front.

'I tell them, "This is your life, and it's ending one minute at a time",' Ivan tells me, before clarifying, '*Fight Club.*'

The light on Ivan's monitor is flashing and as the other three, who I presume take precedence, are all engaged, Ivan pulls on his headset and takes the call with a sigh.

'Yes, I am familiar with that particular item,' Ivan says in his phone voice, shaking muffin crumbs from atop a catalogue on his desk and flicking through the pages, before stopping at one.

'The Lawn Aerator Sandals™ fit any adult shoes. One size does indeed fit all, madam.

'Good – let me process your order. Do you have your credit card details with you? … Might I suggest you also take this opportunity to order a set of replacement spikes? … If the soil underneath your lawn is strongly compacted or contains gravel then they *will* be necessary … Only an additional $29.95 … Good decision.'

Ivan starts punching the order into a template on his computer and nudges me, suggesting I familiarise myself with the catalogue. The catalogue is nearly two hundred pages and contains the greatest array of crap you can imagine.

'Okay,' Ivan says once his customer has been stripped of her excess money, 'our team here is responsible for all phoned queries and orders relating to the Sky Mall catalogue.'

'A new catalogue is printed seasonally,' he continues, 'and letterbox dropped in areas where stupid people live. It's also distributed via the seat pockets on all Virgin Blue domestic flights – hence the name – Sky Mall.'

'Do you get a lot of orders via phone?' I ask – you're meant to ask questions in the beginning.

'Mostly older people who don't like ordering online and anyone who has questions before they cave in to an item's charms.'

'So, how do you answer all their questions?'

'Mostly it's just restating the information that's in the catalogue. That usually does the trick. However, you can put the item number into this cell and it will bring up any extra selling points the manufacturer has supplied us.'

'Just remember, Grout – this stuff is not made by us so don't take any grief. We just process the orders to the manufacturers who paid to advertise in the catalogue – they have to fulfil it.'

'Cool,' I say.

'And, finally, *they*,' Ivan nods towards the clutch of walled offices, 'monitor our calls and insist we try and upsell one extra item every call. I keep a selection pinned in front of me for easy reference.'

'Okay,' I say, looking at Ivan's favourite upsells. His list appears a little out there.

'Put on this headset and you can listen in on my calls for a bit,' Ivan tells me.

'Hello. I'm calling about the Always Fresh Pet Drinking System™ in your catalogue. On page seventy-one?'

We both flick quickly and Ivan says, 'Yes madam – would you like to order one now?'

'I just want to ask something first. It says in the catalogue that the canine one is $79.95 and the feline one is $59.95?'

'That's right, madam – the canine one holds more water.'

'My dog is real small – will feline do for him?'

'Do you want your dog to get a complex?'

I have to pull my headset off as I start to laugh but Ivan maintains his straight face and even upsells the lady a Pet Ramp and Staircase™, which he explains, 'unlike lesser pet staircases that are difficult to climb for arthritic or older pets, this item converts into a ramp, providing pets with access to sofas or beds without exerting as much strain on joints and muscles'.

Flashing light. Click. 'Welcome to Sky Mall. This is Ivan.'

'Can you tell me which size RealRock™ I require?'

We both head to the index, in perfect synchronicity, and find the double-page spread devoted to these plastic rocks that 'are replicated from rocks in nature, hollow and lightweight, and make it easy to enhance your yard or cover problem areas in your landscape'. Moreover, 'four flanges let you secure each fake rock into the ground and they come in six styles: mini, jumbo, short, long, tall, and super'.

'I've got a pool filter,' the guy adds while we get up to speed.

'You'll need the super,' Ivan says authoritatively.

'Okay – I'll order a super please.'

'Fieldstone grey or riverbed brown?'

Ivan and the guy settle on the grey; Ivan explains to the customer, and me, what he reckons a flange is, and then he covers his microphone and says, 'I'll make him an offer he can't refuse,' before pitching the Portable Wooden Pathway™ that 'keeps your feet from getting muddy while you're working in the garden'.

Over the next few calls Ivan processes orders for a GPS Personal Location Finder™ – in case you can't find your car or simply don't know where you are; a $49.95 Deluxe Bagel Slicer™ – which achieves nothing more than a breadknife can manage quite effectively; and, most impressively, a Roadmaster Passenger Seat Office™ – a 'workstation that straps to the seat next to the driver, with the existing seat belt, and provides a nonslip writing surface, hanging file section and space for a laptop and accessories. An optional printer stand mounts to the top corner.' The catalogue suggests it's not for use while driving.

I feel like applauding at the end and then wonder what the fuck is wrong with me.

'Let's get you going solo,' Ivan declares and I claim my own segment of the pod, lay out my catalogue, set my screen up and await a call.

'At my signal, unleash hell,' Ivan the Gladiator says and I click the flashing light.

The caller directs me to the page that features the Birdwatcher's Motion Activated Camera™ – 'a weather-resistant digital camera that detects motion and automatically snaps pictures of birds and other wildlife – up to twenty pictures in twenty seconds. It mounts to windows, walls, posts, or trees (mounting accessories provided) and you can direct the camera at birdbaths or feeders.'

'So, can you clarify,' the bloke asks, 'it will take photos while I sleep so I don't have to be there myself to see the possums and owls and whatnot?'

'The whatnot will be a surprise for you each morning,' I say and Ivan gives me the thumbs-up.

'Perfect. I'll take it.'

'Great. Can I direct you to page forty-one of your catalogue?' I ask, not entirely sure what I'm about to recommend but I've trained with the master so here goes. 'You may find our very popular SkyRest Travel Pillow™ of interest.'

This thing inflates to a ridiculous size and sits on your tray during a flight.

'Won't I look kinda like an idiot?' the guy asks.

'I guess so,' I say and we stick with the idiotic digital camera that chooses what to shoot all by itself.

'That pillow is a hard sell,' Ivan assures me. 'Let's take an early lunch – there's a cafeteria upstairs.'

'Okay.'

Ivan leans over the pod towards Mason, Shearer and Weaver before announcing, 'I'll be back.'

The cafeteria has a reasonable selection of tepid snacks and we take a table as near the windows as possible.

'So, where do you live, Grout?'

'In the city – Swanston Street,' I reply. 'And you?'

'Ascot Vale.'

'Oh, I have friends, um, family, sort of, in North Melbourne. Not too far from you, roughly, I think.'

'I'm glad you make more sense when you're on a call,' Ivan says kindly and I laugh.

Ivan has bought his *Herald Sun* with him and, pausing in the entertainment section on a page featuring a celebrity with an explosion of tits, says to me with a considered expression, 'I can't jerk off to magazine or newspaper images. It's so static. And naked – that's even less likely to get me hard. I prefer my imagination.'

'Fair enough,' I say.

'Friends, colleagues or celebrities?' Ivan asks me, as if this is the most likely question to throw someone you've just met.

'It depends,' I say. Some mates go a lifetime without the masturbation discussion and here we are, fresh acquaintances, into it within hours.

'I can't wank to someone I don't know,' Ivan says thoughtfully and finally turns the page and his mind flips as well – to the topic of rising street violence in the city. Soon he'll have read all the way to the front page.

'Someone has to die in order that the rest of us should value life more,' Ivan mutters, shaking his head at the attack on a Dutch tourist.

Just like that – switching from his preferred method of jerking off to quoting Virginia Woolf in *The Hours*.

We return to our pod just in time to replace two of our teammates who are dying for their go at the remaining selection of pre-packaged food substitutes. The lady remains, enjoying the peace of not a single call currently being in play.

'Mason, this is Grout,' Ivan says. 'Grout has family in North Melbourne. He thinks.'

Why is that such an issue? Let's talk about masturbation.

'Mason lives in North Melbourne.'

Oh, now I get it.

Mason says to me, 'I don't know any Grouts.'

'Their name is Lever,' I say, sticking with the surname theme so as not to freak anyone out.

'Travis Lever?' Mason comes to life. I wouldn't have been surprised if she knew Joy – she's probably only a few years adrift of her – but Travis?

'He's my brother.' I remove the step for once – to give it a test run. See if it fits.

Mason looks me up and down – requiring less head movement than doing the same to Travis would – before saying sceptically, 'I *suppose* there is some resemblance.'

'Step,' I add.

'That makes sense.'

I remember the lady who was sitting outside the house when I dropped off the letter for Joy. So far as I recall, she looked different to this one.

'How's he doing?'

'Fine,' I say.

'Does he still collect for the Red Cross?'

'While I've known him he's been a model,' I reply, presuming that's how she came to be agog over Travis.

'Oh, that's a pity. Travis was a great collector.'

I'm just about done with Mason's starry eyes so I jump on the next incoming call. I recognise the number that displays on the monitor and it's the guy who'd ordered the camera that takes in the sights while you sleep. He wants to make sure that batteries are included.

Through the afternoon I shift a cat litterbox that is hidden within an elegant bathroom cabinet – the illustration in the catalogue shows how neatly the shit-scoop hangs beside the guest towel; a handbag insert that allows you to move the contents from one bag to another without the fuss of having to transfer everything individually – that caller paid extra for monogramming; and the biggest item was a Carcoon™ – whose 'patented Active Airflow and Carbon Filtration Systems create a clean, dry and controlled atmosphere around your vehicle – with dust, moisture and other corrosives removed'. This was worth $999 to someone.

I stuck with upselling the same item each time – a barbecue branding tool which enables the entertainer in you to personalise your steaks, chicken and even burgers with up to three initials.

Two callers took the fries with their order.

All the while Ivan would occasionally offer me guidance and even instant-messaged me at one point with, *They may take away our lives, but they'll never take our freedom!*

With the sun dipping and the call rate tapering off, it occurs to me that the thought of flogging this stuff another day might set in motion a process whereby I end up like Ivan. Nice guy as he is, I don't need stir-crazy. That, combined with the fact I found myself in the last hour considering how I might take advantage of the staff discount on some of this rubbish, has me pretty much decided.

I'm so close to flying … I can taste it.

Huh? Ivan messages me back.

The Fantastic Four.

19. The Land of the Giants

'Hey – it's just Ethan. I'm not sure if that launch party is still on tomorrow, but anyway, you can call me back if you want or it's fine if not or there's no spare ticket or whatever. Did I say it's just Ethan?'

As a trial run for calling Alejandra my shot with Travis has proven that I *can* make a call. However, this doesn't mean I will be even partway lucid.

My mobile rings.

'Hi, it's Travis!'

I wait for the *Tah-dah!*

'Hey, that was quick,' I say out loud.

'I dropped my phone when you called,' Travis tells me. 'So you're still on for tomorrow – unreal.'

'I guess so – if that's still okay?'

'Of course. I was going to call – you beat me to it.'

That's a first.

'So,' Travis says, 'I'll put your name on the door and if there's any problem just get them to come find me.'

'Ah, okay,' I say, suddenly planning not to front.

Travis must sense the hesitancy in my voice. 'Don't back out, Ethan – it'll be fun.'

'Yeah. No. Of course,' I ramble. 'So who'll be at this fashion mag launch thingamee?'

'I guess it's mainly about impressing advertising agencies and clients – they want heaps of us models around to give it a mood. There'll also be photographers, stylists, you know the drill.'

The drill I don't know.

Travis gives me the address of the club, which he reckons is as hip as the famous Buddha Bar in Paris except it is in Exhibition Street.

'I'll be there from eleven,' Travis says.

'At night?'

'Funny,' Travis replies. 'See you tomorrow Ethan.'

■ ■ ■

The crowd at Baxter's has never seen me at this time of the evening – let alone heading out, into the darkness. I could be dressed for a job interview if it weren't that I've left my tie out of the ensemble. I *have* brought along the butterflies though.

Weaving through the Swanston Street crowd who'll soon be barfing, bonking and brawling, I arrive at the club in Exhibition Street unscathed. The bogons have thinned out, replaced by a thinner crowd who're less likely to barf on the street but no less familiar with the art of upchucking itself.

My assessment of the clamour of glamour trying to get in is that they are *all* models. The girls work hard to appear ethereal, while the guys struggle with the impossible task of exuding both manliness and lithe fragility simultaneously. Meanwhile, I feel shorter than the stories on *Entertainment Tonight*.

The guy on the door can't understand why Ethan is spelt as it sounds but he relents and lets me pass. It's almost midnight so Travis *has* to be here.

'Hey, you made it!'

Travis appears from amongst the forest of his fellow giants and I instantly feel more at ease.

'I can't believe it – they let *me* in,' I say with a smile, but Travis doesn't know what I mean.

'Your name is on the door,' he assures me.

Through a momentary gap in the crowd I recognise Tatiana, alone and slugging champagne by an ice sculpture of a peacock – apparently the new magazine is called *Peacock*. If it weren't for the rapid movement of Tatiana's flute to her frozen lips, I'd have thought her the less animate of the two.

'Tatiana's over there,' I say to Travis, who has fetched us a mojito each from a wide-eyed waiter.

'Zac's not here yet,' Travis tells me, waving at Tatiana and splashing a drink into my hand.

'Oh well,' I reply.

Tatiana spots Travis – she's unlikely to see me amongst the chests and breasts, even if she did recall my face – but she decides to stay put, beside her more rapidly melting companion.

'So, what's Joy doing tonight?'

'Sleeping,' Travis says. 'She spent the day with a bunch of her friends and is pretty exhausted. She had fun though.'

'Cool,' I say.

'Mum wants you to come over again. Do you ever get out our way?'

'I will,' I tell him.

Silver trays of morsels dance amongst the throng and I take a few things that seem familiar. Travis doesn't eat anything.

'White shirt,' he explains.

'I see.'

'*And* my agent is watching me,' Travis says.

'She doesn't endorse eating?'

'Not so much.'

We both conquer several more mojitos; apparently everyone is convinced there are no calories so long as chewing isn't involved.

Travis is double-cheek kissed by several passers-by and each time, upon being introduced, I'd ask how they got into modelling and invariably they claim to have been cajoled into it by family or friends.

After telling each of them 'Zac's not here yet', Travis's attempts at prolonged conversations with the social butterflies falters and pretty soon their eyes begin to wander and they dart off to continue the double-cheek kissing marathon. Amongst his peers Travis doesn't seem as widely accepted as I'd expected. Like Diner's Club. He's not alone though – it's as if all the models are so magnetised they are at once attracted to and repelled by each other. The fact that he is probably the best looking of the guys in the crowd won't help his chances bonding with the males in this world.

'How did *you* get into modelling?' I ask Travis. 'Was it Joy's idea?'

'Nope, I thought it might be fun.'

Somewhere there are speeches going on but interest in *Peacock* amongst the peacocks is zero. The Silver Fox comes by and says hello. He has altered his skin colour and positively glows. The model with him seems, momentarily, to presume I'm one of them and this causes me to wonder if I might appear hotter in cooler lighting.

'You have a really different look,' she tells me.

It's called ordinary.

'Thanks. I guess,' I say.

She smiles kindly and, after advising that 'my friend sent my photo to a modelling agency as a joke and now here I am', takes her leave.

'Zac's not here yet,' Travis tells the Silver Fox, though I don't know if, in all the noise, TSF actually asked after Zac or Travis just assumed he did.

Whilst the Silver Fox explains to me what exactly a creative director does, Zac finally arrives, entering the club with the confidence and swagger of one hitting the sunshine after liberally applying a coat of SPF50.

He briefly acknowledges our existence before pushing his lips around the crowd for a bit. On rejoining us, Zac casts a severe eye over the Silver Fox and says, 'Siimon, you do realise it's not summer yet?'

'I like to be ahead of the crowd,' Siimon replies, seemingly not offended.

'You are *well* ahead,' Zac says.

Next it'll be Travis's turn no doubt.

'Should you be wearing that colour with food around?'

Travis studies his crisp and very expensive-looking white shirt, and replies with a winning smile, 'All clear so far.'

How Zac must resent that smile.

'Congratulations,' Zac says.

'The food's a little slow anyway,' I say, trying to distract Zac from his rounds.

Zac doesn't look at me but nods at Travis, whilst smiling for the benefit of Siimon,

'Well, it's not a particularly fast crowd.'

Travis either misses or ignores the inference, so I suck it up. It's not my place.

'What are you up to tomorrow?' Zac asks Siimon.

'Tanning salon.'

'You're kidding?'

'*You* could do with a bit of colour actually, Zac – you're looking somewhat vampiric,' Siimon replies.

'I'll be laughing when I'm your age,' Zac says.

'Laughing won't help those lines,' Siimon points at Zac's unlined face.

Eventually the old fox and the young vampire shift into the crowd and I tell Travis thanks for the invite but I'm going to head home.

'I might too,' Travis says. 'I've got a booking for tomorrow – I'm busting out a new line of jeans.'

'Good for you,' I say.

It's far easier getting out of the club than in and I'm amazed to see people are still arriving.

'I'll get a cab from Swanston Street,' Travis tells me and we start walking. Each time people headed in the other direction pass between us their gazes follow Travis but he seems oblivious.

'So how did that call centre thing work out?' Travis asks me.

'I lasted a day,' I reply. 'But the guy I worked with put me on to his local pub that apparently always needs staff and is none too worried about certificates.'

'What pub?'

'He called it the Valey.'

'The Valley?'

'No. The Valey. Ascot Vale.'

'Have you worked in a pub before?' Travis asks me.

'No,' I say, acknowledging, 'I guess living in one might not cut it.'

'Don't worry,' Travis tells me, 'it's easy. You'll be fine.'

'I'm not sure my reference from Auto World is gonna help.'

'Give them my number. I can be the bar manager from Baxter's,' Travis says.

'Really?'

'Sure.'

'Cheers.'

'Hey Ethan – feel like getting kebabs?'

'What about your white shirt?' I ask.

'Doesn't matter,' Travis says. 'It's just you.'

20. Perfume on a Pig

'See you tomorrow then Ethan.'

'Okay. Thanks heaps.'

Joy is certainly persistent. I look at my mobile – I could just as easily call Alejandra immediately and invite her along for dinner as instructed, but I won't. Not yet. I'll leave it to the last possible minute, if at all. When you meet someone and they already have a life, aren't they just passing traffic and aren't you meant to know that?

My mobile rings again – twice in one night – causing Mister Fantastic to jump also.

■ ■ ■

'See you tomorrow then Ethan.'

'Okay. Thanks heaps.'

Logan was actually impressed. I look at my mobile – I could just as easily call Travis immediately and thank him for the winning reference but I won't. Not yet. I'll wait until tomorrow night – once I've lasted a day at the Valey and survive for another, unlike my last job. Meanwhile I have to go downstairs and study the bar staff

132

doing their stuff so I've some hope of living up to whatever it is Travis promised my new boss.

■ ■ ■

The Valey is much smaller than Baxter's but, given its slightly remote location, likely provides way more square-metreage per customer. There are a few tables out front, a few pool tables inside, and too few staff apparently. I stand at the bar and wait to spot any form of life. Eventually a guy with facial hair inspired by the Taliban comes out from a door behind the bar area and sees me.

'What would you like?'

'My job,' I say. 'I'm Ethan.'

Logan introduces himself and shakes my hand.

'Come round and meet the staff.'

The staff is Seth.

Seth looks like a Sex Pistol – the band that is: pale, skinny and spotty. The three of us stand in the small kitchen behind the bar area while Seth, sitting on the massive deep freezer as if trying to keep the corpses from escaping, struggles to maintain eye contact, let alone conversation. His long, lank hair is of a colour not found in nature – in here, however, it most closely resembles the chicken stock.

'Seth is a graduate from TAFE,' Logan announces. 'He *is* a cook.'

Logan seems to be trying to convince himself that this quiet and unassuming young guy, just old enough to be served a drink, shares his qualifications with Jamie Oliver and Gordon Ramsay.

'It's just you and Seth on during the day – so you need to help each other out when one or the other is busy,' Logan tells me.

And when we're both busy?

'Don't worry though,' Logan adds, 'I'll be in and out as well.'

We leave Seth to pick at his face in peace and Logan runs me through the layout of the bar and the intricacies of the cash register.

It's still midmorning so we're rarely interrupted by customers and I'm hoping I won't have to pour my first beer while Logan is in.

'Now, Ethan, with your previous management skills, you are in charge whilst I'm not here.'

What, exactly, did Travis say to Logan?

'And, of course, given your experience with the food side, please feel free to offer some guidance to Seth if you believe his menu can do with a bit of jazzing up.'

My food experience?

'I was very impressed with Mr Lever. Travis,' Logan says. 'We share similar views on hospitality and what it takes to succeed in this business.'

Seems Travis is *very* impressive. So far I've seen loads of folk bowled over by him but I've always credited that to his looks. Maybe Zac's the one who is as clueless as a Melbourne weather forecaster.

'I was quite taken ...'

You certainly were.

'... with his thoughts and I might even call into Baxter's at some point so we can share some more ideas about this crazy industry of ours ...'

Oh fuck Travis, too much.

'... Travis told me you fairly lived at that place.'

'That's no lie,' I say.

'Dedication like that will get you somewhere in this life,' Logan says, misting up.

'All seems pretty straightforward,' I say, hoping to divert my new boss from continuing to dwell on the wisdom of my 'old' one.

'Just call me on my mobile if there are any problems,' Logan tells me and is gone.

As soon as Logan has left, Seth wanders out of the kitchen and waits for me to strike up a chat.

'Do you like it here?' I ask him.

With new colleagues, as opposed to other new acquaintances,

the familiar territory of *what do you do?* isn't an option so you gotta go with *how do you do?*

'It's okay – pretty quiet,' Seth says quietly.

'So, what's on the lunch menu?' I ask cheerfully.

Seth points at the menu board glumly. There are all the standards and then some – from nachos with all the trimmings to three different cuts of steak.

'Do we offer all of that?'

'We offer it but that doesn't mean we have it,' Seth replies.

'What do you do if someone orders something we don't have?' I ask.

'We either say "it's run out" or I have to run out,' Seth says.

'Huh?'

'If it's too early in the day to say we've run out I have to run to the IGA and get it.'

'How come we don't just buy it in beforehand?'

'Logan likes to run a tight ship,' Seth warns me.

'Do you have to run to the shop that often?'

'Often enough.'

No wonder he's as skinny as the zambuca bottle.

Given the authority designated to me by my new boss I suggest we rummage through the freezer so we might save Seth from running himself out of the leftover body he has remaining.

Under the bags of fries and nuggets, there is a layer of pre-prepared parmas.

'Our dream is a day where everyone orders a parma and fries,' Seth says wistfully, his tired legs relaxing at the mere thought of it.

'What's this?' I ask, tapping on a great lump of something that's wedged deep in the freezer.

Seth hits the thing with his fist.

'I think it's a turkey.'

'Maybe we can do a Thanksgiving special in November?' I suggest creatively.

'It'll take till then to thaw,' Seth says and we leave the thing under the wave of parmas.

'Shop!'

Someone's at the bar.

We both head out for the company. It's a guy with a broad smile and light blue eyes that are more normally wed to blond hair. He hasn't shaved in a bit.

'I'm Andrew,' the guy says to me, then nodding at Seth, 'I know this little fella, but I haven't seen you before?'

'I'm Ethan. I started today.'

'Welcome to the Valey, son,' Andrew says, though he's barely ten years older than me.

'What would you like?'

'Three jugs and three pot glasses,' Seth predicts.

'Got it in one,' Andrew says with a wink and I realise it's me ordering my 52.

'What do you recommend for lunch, buddy?' Andrew asks Seth.

'You guys never eat,' Seth replies.

'True enough,' Andrew admits.

While they're busy mixing it up I set about pouring the beer into the jugs, hoping they won't notice my shaking hands. In the beginning I pull the lever on the tap too cautiously and it sprays about a bit and Seth leans over and sets me right.

Once the three jugs are done I offer to carry the glasses to the table out front where Andrew's mates are sitting.

'Take a break if you like,' Seth tells me. 'I'm going to start on mixing the wretched sauces and boiling the long-time cooked vegetables.'

And I thought my attitude stank.

The sun is hitting the front area and I place the glasses on the inhabited table. A guy I assume is much the same age as Andrew, though he looks a hell of a lot rougher for the journey, gives me a smile of decay. I thought alcohol was used to preserve things? There is also a grandmotherly-type woman with glasses so thick

I assume she's blind well before starting in on her first jug. Two dogs with patches of mange pick about their feet.

'Sit down, Ethan,' Andrew says and I'm sort of stuck since he's heard Seth suggest I take a break from the fatigue caused by pouring three jugs.

Andrew doesn't introduce the other two as such and I can't show him up by asking their names in case he doesn't recall them or never knew them in the first place. The nameless guy looks well wired, more than could be credited by alcohol alone. The old lady smiles at my blurry image as Andrew offers me some of his jug – which I pass on. I'm aware that there is a couple at a table just inside, but they seem content watching the plasma.

'So, Ethan, what brings you to work here?'

'The tram.'

'Very funny,' Andrew says, and then seriously, 'I wanted to be a comedian once.'

The freaky guy and the old lady both laugh, the dogs aren't that bothered.

'See, I'm *that* good,' Andrew says cheerfully.

I want to ask what brings him here, every day by the sound of it, watching the world go by until, presumably, he can't see anything at all.

The old lady tries to pat one of the dogs on its head but ends up lashing out at thin air.

'So, anyone special in your life?' Andrew asks me.

'Nope,' I say. I used to say 'not yet' to that question.

'I *was* married,' Andrew tells me, with the confiding nature that comes about during the rapid displacement of a jug's contents.

'Not any more?' I ask needlessly.

'His wife left him – pregnant with their first,' the messier-looking guy tells me before he wonders out loud why one of the dogs keeps staring at him. Probably a sniffer dog.

Andrew doesn't seem to mind that his tale of woe has been leaked by his mate. In fact, as I think of what I might say to comfort

Andrew, the other two divulge their résumés: *she* hasn't been able to sleep since being mugged for her handbag by someone she's no hope of describing to the police; and *he* has been diagnosed with a liver complaint – no prizes for guessing which one.

Inside I can see Seth taking a food order from the only other people in the joint – who've been watching *Oprah* reruns on cable all this time when just outside we have free-to-air, live *Oprah Platinum* on offer.

The drinking buddies are setting about getting gold coins together to finance their next round, the old lady leaving it to the other two to tell her how much she's contributed to the communal fund, when Seth dashes past me, pausing long enough to shout, 'Pork!'

I walk with Andrew back inside.

'How long have you been a regular here?' I ask.

'Too long already.'

It's barely four hours and I feel the same.

Andrew continues, 'I just hate going home to an empty house and sitting there, my mind ticking away faster than the clock. It takes beer to get me to passing out, which is as nice a place as I can visit at the moment. I'll get through it, though, I reckon.' It would all sound so miserable if it weren't served with a genuine smile and some sense of hope: a couple of sides that would better most anything in the kitchen here.

After Seth returns and starts grilling the two pieces of pork he found down the street he tells me to 'liven up' the apple sauce. This requires, apparently, skimming the surface, shaving some ice frosting from out of the freezer and mixing it in with a squeeze of lemon juice and some sugar. Lots of mixing.

'Who orders pork?' Seth complains.

'It's on the menu board,' I say.

'There's too much choice,' Seth says.

'Less is more and all that,' I offer.

'Exactly!' Seth agrees, coming alive faster than the apple sauce all of a sudden. 'We should create a few really special things.'

'You could have a point,' I say.

I deposit Seth's creations in front of the couple inside and the guy inspects his pork with a spoon – as if peeling roadkill off tarmac with a shovel.

He says to his girlfriend, 'I need some perfume to put on this pig.'

She passes the jugette of *livened* apple sauce.

Outside drunk o'clock has come and gone; the conversation gets louder even though its blindness they're battling, not deafness.

Logan stays clear of the place my entire shift, appearing exactly at knock-off time.

'How'd you go, Ethan?'

'It was very *mellow*.' He may not want to hear the word 'quiet'. 'But no problems,' I add.

'Well, we'll see you tomorrow.'

'Okay,' I say, and pop into the kitchen to farewell Seth who is stuck doing prep for his night-time replacement.

'See you tomorrow buddy,' I say.

'Yeah.'

'Why don't you haul out that turkey? It can defrost overnight.'

'Really?' Seth looks confused.

'Let's put it to use.'

'You're the boss.'

That really doesn't sit easily but what the hey.

'See you, Andrew,' I say to the only member of the outside posse not completely under the table. Yet.

'See you tomorrow, Ethan,' Andrew says like he's a co-worker.

I stop for a moment, on my own time, and say to him, 'I'm going to call this girl tonight – Alejandra. Ask her along to a dinner party.'

'Good on you,' Andrew says. 'Good luck with that.'

'Cheers.'

21. Just Ethan

All those people in my dad's life – he hadn't just run into them on his endless string of jobs and left it at that. He brought them along with him. Dad gathered friends like someone picking flowers – choosing any he'd like to share his space with before moving on to the next garden.

'Hello?'

'Hey. It's just Ethan.'

'Oh. Hi, Ethan – your name didn't come up for some reason,' Alejandra says.

'If you're busy I can call back at some other –'

'I *am* busy – busy trying to ignore the television. Damien signed us up for a hundred channels – said it would be good company. I don't want any of them in my house.'

I'm guessing he's in another room.

'Well, I just thought I'd ring and say hello …'

'I didn't think you'd call. I like surprises.'

'… and ask you, Joy – you remember my stepmother – Joy wants to ask if you'd like to come for dinner at her place?'

'When?'

'Tomorrow night.'

I did leave it too late.

'Let's see – I've got a Foxtel guide here – Tuesday night. I don't know, Ethan, you're up against some pretty solid competition. Oh, okay – you're on.'

'Yes?'

'Yes!'

'Cool – Joy really took a shine to you.'

'She's nice,' Alejandra says. 'So give me the address and I'll see you tomorrow night.'

■ ■ ■

Outside the town hall clock is still refusing to budge; and inside, my 52 tastes the same as always – but maybe something has changed. Dinner tomorrow is *so* going to beat a pub lunch – turkey or no turkey.

■ ■ ■

'What time did you tell her?' Joy asks, basting her thighs again.

'I just said dinner,' I reply, starting to worry.

'It's fine, Ethan. Trav isn't home yet either,' Joy says, then, 'Look at your face!'

'I've got an insider's view thanks,' I say.

'Tell me more about this pub job.'

'Well, it's real quiet and there's me and the cook – Seth. The boss, Logan, didn't even turn up today.'

'So, just you and Seth – that's it?' Joy asks, while trying to locate a particular appliance amongst her Cash Convertors display of crap in the overflowing kitchen cabinets.

'Not really – the regulars are very … regular. I see more of them than the boss.'

'What are they like?' Joy removes a tagine and sets a yoghurt maker aside so she can shift the bread machine out of the way of the rice cooker.

'They drink steadily but we fed them some turkey for lunch today.'

'That should slow them down,' Joy says.

'Can I help?' I ask again.

'Thanks, Ethan, but I've done this a thousand times.'

'How are you doing anyway?'

I have to go there even if she brushes me off.

'I'm doing fine. Really. I get tired but then I sleep – anyone could do it,' Joy says cheerfully but then a flicker of concern betrays her tone.

'What?' I ask.

'I do worry about Trav, though – he's too young to be stuck here looking after me,' Joys says.

'From what I can tell, there's no place he'd rather be,' I say, then pointing at the simmering feast, 'and meanwhile, I'm not sure who's looking after whom here.'

'Thanks Ethan.'

'Thank you,' I say.

'Oh, by the way, it's Trav's birthday next week,' Joy tells me.

'Oh cool,' I say, not sure if that involves me in any way.

'He's going to have drinks at this little bar in the city he loves and ask all his mates. I'm sure you'll be part of that.'

'If he wants me there.'

'You've met some of his friends, haven't you?'

'Sure have,' I say.

'Zac's a prat but Trav seems to idolise him,' Joy says. 'I hope he gets a turnout.'

'I wouldn't worry – I've seen Travis scrolling through a phone list as never-ending as the movie credits for *Lord of the Rings*,' I tell Joy, not mentioning the envy it's stirred in me.

'Sometimes less is more,' Joy says, and I think about the menu board Seth has to deal with.

There's a knock on the door.

Joy looks at me. 'Trav doesn't knock.'

Diego and I head down the hall.

'Hi,' Alejandra says, fetchingly attired in a simple black dress and carrying a bottle of wine.

'Hi,' I say. 'Oh, let me introduce the *other* Diego.'

'I like *this* one,' Alejandra jokes, shaking his little paw. 'Not as yappy as mine.'

Joy has no hesitation in hugging Alejandra and just as they are reacquainting I hear Travis come through the front door.

'Hi everyone,' Travis says, pulling a compact black case that has two wheels and a long metallic handle. The case has his name embossed on the top.

'Not my idea,' Travis notes me looking at the thing. 'All the models in the agency get one of these to haul our stuff about in. I feel like an airline steward.'

'Trav – this is Alejandra,' Joy says from her perch on a kitchen stool.

I suddenly realise I've forgotten to worry ahead of time that either Alejandra or Travis might be taken with the other, or both, but from what I can sense I'd have wasted my time. Woo-hoo!

'What's for dinner?' Travis asks his mother whilst heading towards his bedroom.

'Tandoori chicken,' Joy calls out after him and, turning to Alejandra who has sat herself on the other kitchen stool and is opening the wine, notes, 'Ethan loves chicken.'

Travis, used to changing in a matter of seconds, returns wearing torn jeans and a luminescent orange T-shirt. He sits next to me on the sofa and we split the loving that's on offer from Diego.

'So, Ethan, did you get that pub job?' Travis asks me.

'Sure did – thanks for the reference by the way.'

'No worries.'

I fill Travis in on this week's job and he tells me about the plans for his birthday drinks. All the while I attempt to keep an ear on things that might be boiling along in the kitchen.

'... first time was back when Trav was still quite young. Ovarian. They took them out, of course, and after a while I thought I'd beaten it for good. Late at night, after Trav had gone to bed and I was finishing off his homework, I'd occasionally let myself worry that I'd stopped worrying but mostly I considered it dealt with.'

I watch Alejandra put her arm around Joy's thin frame.

'This time around the first thing I did was give up doing Sudoku – why kill my remaining time?' Joy says to Alejandra.

How do women do this? Not just the listening in on two conversations simultaneously, but the getting straight to the heart of things on barely half a glass of wine each.

'Zac reckons he'll come and there are heaps of others from the agency. I'm doing invites via Facebook as well.' Back to Travis.

'Sounds like quite a crowd ...'

Perfect to get lost in.

'You'll definitely be there?' Travis asks.

'Definitely,' I say, actually meaning it.

'Your folks called you Joy Lever?' Alejandra asks with a smile.

'It was a more innocent time,' Joy replies with a grin. 'Maybe I should have taken Ethan's father's name.'

'Grout?' Alejandra says.

'Huh?' I call out from the sofa, pretending like I'm not listening in.

'Nothing,' both Joy and Alejandra call out in unison.

'So after freezing outside all morning in board shorts, I then have to do an indoor shoot, under stinking hot lights. Cashmere coats, scarves, a friggin' dinner suit!' Travis recounts his day at the office.

'And I complain about pouring a few jugs of beer,' I say.

'... ignore him – you look great,' Joy tells Alejandra. 'I wish I'd started with a bit more weight on me.'

'I got to keep the board shorts!' Travis says. 'Four pairs!'

'What about the dinner suit?'

'I hope never to have use for one,' Travis says. Maybe we are related.

'… and it would be a waste to spend money on new clothes,' Joy is saying. 'I'm even using up all the remnants of makeup I have. Look at me going green!'

'The thing is, we're working so far ahead – the boardies shoot was for next year's northern spring/summer and the other was for fall/winter after that – global warming might have claimed us all by then.'

'So you can do all this stuff for another hemisphere whilst remaining based in Melbourne?' I ask Travis, who has won Diego's undivided affection now.

'My agency wants me to shift to New York for a bit,' Travis replies, 'when, things get better here.'

I put my arm around his shoulder but I can't assure him that things will get better here.

'She'll be okay,' Travis says quietly – to me or himself, I'm not sure which.

In the kitchen there is a definite smell of burning and Joy pulls the tray of chicken parts out of the oven. Even from here I can see they're blacker than Alejandra's wardrobe.

'I used to be such a good cook,' she cries, defeated. 'Well, adequate at least.'

'No worries. Just say it's Cajun,' Alejandra says matter-of-factly, and sets about scraping the chicken down.

'Trav – change your shirt – it's no longer tandoori,' Joy calls out, laughing with tears, and ferrying the food.

'I'll risk it,' Travis says, cheering up, and we take our places at the table.

'Maybe you shouldn't,' Joy says, cutting into a piece and striking blood.

'Who feels like burgers?' Travis says.

'I'm sorry, guys,' Joy tells us, looking weary all of a sudden.

'You relax here, Mum – we'll just go up the street and fetch some stuff,' Travis says false-brightly as he sets Joy down on the sofa.

■ ■ ■

'So, Alejandra, what do you do?' Travis asks as we walk towards the shops, all partaking in her ciggie to varying degrees: Alejandra wholeheartedly, Travis an occasional puff and me all passive.

'I'm starting a job at a publishing company – Tate Lane – next week,' Alejandra says.

Oh, man, I should have asked her about the interview!

'What's the job?' Travis asks.

'I'm the assistant to one of the publishers – dealing with the incoming manuscripts mostly, I think.'

Outside the fish and chip shop a V8-load of hoodies is just pulling up so Travis suggests we step lively. 'If they order before us it'll take ages.'

We order three burgers and a cardboard skip of fried stuff whilst Alejandra discusses the other menu options with the lady behind the counter. As we wait for it all to be rushed through the cooking process, Travis eyes the ready-already stack of dim sims.

'They look good – I might have one while we're here,' Travis says, and orders a blistered chunk.

'Nice,' he says, offering us both a bite, and getting to keep it all to himself.

One of the bogons from outside comes in and orders enough food to fill the car out front, let alone just the stomachs of those sheltering inside it.

'I told you,' Travis tells us.

'Oh, can I have a couple of those,' the bogon asks the lady, pointing at the stack of dim sims, 'for my dog.'

Alejandra laughs so loud I can barely make out the fryers for a few seconds.

We leave with the sweating bags of food and pass a DVD store.

'Maybe we should get a DVD?' I say, not sure if that will sound antisocial – but I always worry about conversation running out.

'Good idea – I'm a member here,' Travis says and we go inside.

We all stand in front of the New Releases shelves for a bit, our heads scrolling up and down as if we're facing Jerusalem's Wailing Wall, before Travis makes for a section that seems entirely devoted to Seth Rogen comedies, and we follow.

'Hey, I just remembered something,' I say to Travis. 'Joy told me, the other time I came for dinner, that she wished she'd gotten to Japan, so ...'

I pluck the copy of *Lost in Translation* from a shelf.

'... what about this?'

'Done,' Travis says.

We detour into the IGA as Travis reckons there's something he's been meaning to pick up for Joy for a while. He dashes down an aisle, like Seth must have to do each time someone orders something other than a parma at the Valey, and Alejandra and I hold a spot in the line. Obviously we check out the contents of the hand-baskets of the people ahead of us.

At the top of the line a couple of optimistic guys in skinny jeans prepare for their night out with a purchase of breath mints and condoms. Immediately in front of us a leotarded woman's basket is all skimmed milk and pitted prunes.

I'm about to say, *Life's too short*, but recall in time that Alejandra likely buys the same depressing stuff.

'Life's too short,' Travis says, joining us and observing our eyes on the basket of health.

Alejandra appears to be lost in thoughts of her own so I shift the conversation.

'What'd you get for Joy?' I ask Travis.

Travis shows me a large bottle of expensive-looking women's moisturiser.

'When you are running low, you replenish,' Travis says. 'That's how it goes.'

22. Cold Turkey

'How's Big Bird lasting?'

'We've still got enough for today,' Seth tells me. 'Four days – not bad.'

'What else is good?' I ask with a smile.

'Keep pushing the parmas,' Seth replies.

Logan joins us in the kitchen.

'A table of office workers are about to order,' he warns Seth.

'Parmas,' Seth tells Logan.

I return with Logan to the bar just as a very familiar face walks into the place. Alejandra.

She smiles at me quickly but, seeing my boss, acts like she doesn't know me.

'How can I help you?' Logan asks her whilst I just stand there like a dufus.

'I might get some lunch,' Alejandra tells us.

'Can I suggest the parma?' Logan says.

Suggest all you like, she's so *not* going to order that.

Alejandra scans the menu board. 'I'll have a garden salad.'

Meanwhile a couple of the office workers have wandered up to the bar.

'We'd like to order three parmas ...'

Excellent.

'... and the turkey.'

'We don't have turkey,' Logan says, looking across to the menu board that he fully knows hasn't changed in years.

'I had it the other day – some guy out front recommended it,' one of the office workers says.

'It's a special,' I tell Logan.

Logan looks at me as if to say, *What the fuck?*

'Go on then, give Seth the orders,' Logan tells me, so I have to leave Alejandra out there without a word between us.

I return as quickly as possible but Logan is still lingering about and Alejandra has had to take a table – close enough so she can continue to grin at me living my life.

Andrew arrives from his table outside – looking a little brighter than when I first met him – and I start to pour some jugs.

'We'll get our turkey when you're ready,' Andrew says to me.

Logan looks at me and declares in a low voice, 'They *never* eat.'

I say nothing.

Seth comes around with the garden salad and before I have a chance to take it off him and deliver it myself, Logan says to Seth, none too quietly this time, 'The fat chick.'

I ignore Andrew, who continues to count out his coins, and look over at Alejandra – who has all her senses, unlike the old woman Andrew drinks with. She shrugs her shoulders at me.

Seth, meanwhile, looks lost. He walks in Alejandra's direction, then right past her, depositing the salad in front of a not particularly large woman at the table of office workers.

'We didn't order this,' the woman says.

Alejandra motions to Seth and he brings the salad back over to her.

'Thanks,' Alejandra says kindly. 'Thanks very much.'

Andrew picks up the jugs. 'I'll come back for the glasses ... and the chessboard.'

Logan again gives me a weird look but is suddenly distracted by his mobile.

'I've got to go – not sure when I'll be back,' he tells me, hoping to keep us on edge till he returns.

As soon as he's gone I sit down with Alejandra.

'So, what brings you here?'

'This is my regular,' Alejandra says with a grin.

'Oh, so you'd normally hang with the gang out front then?'

'Sure – we go way back,' Alejandra says.

Seth comes over to me. 'Turkey time?'

'Okay,' I say, and then, 'Seth – this is Alejandra.'

They 'Hey' each other.

I fetch the platter of turkey from the kitchen and say to Alejandra, 'Want to come meet Andrew?'

'Sure.'

We all sit out front and watch as Andrew plays chess with dodgy-liver guy. The old lady most likely can't even see the chessboard, let alone discriminate between a pawn and a king. The three of them don't seem to have tired of the turkey yet and the old lady tells Alejandra her tale of being mugged – which I've heard more times this week than, 'A pint of Carlton thanks.'

'How old do you think I am?' Andrew asks Alejandra for no apparent reason.

'How old do you think you are?'

'I'm nearly forty, and nothing to show for it.'

Alejandra doesn't fall for this shit. 'So, you've got a long way to go then?'

'Huh?' Andrew muses. 'I hadn't thought of it that way.'

Glass half full.

■ ■ ■

Each time anyone approaches the bar I jump up and serve them before returning as quickly as I can manage. The jugs on the table are empty but Andrew and his mates don't seem to notice. I think the old lady is asleep. The windows to her soul are definitely closed behind those thick glasses of hers.

Seth dashes out, but doesn't keep running past us this time. 'There's a scene!'

I follow him back inside, and Alejandra follows me.

'Where's the fucking sour cream?' Some wide-necked, red-faced guy is looking at his nachos wanting to see a white splosh of calories to top off the green, red and yellow ones. 'I told this pretzel stick three times already!'

'I gave him extra guacamole,' Seth tells me as we stand there looking at the quite respectable heap of colours.

'It says sour cream!' the guy says, swinging a fat hand in the direction of the menu board.

'We'll just check the kitchen,' I say to the guy in the hope of diffusing the situation, and the three of us stand around the freezer looking at each other.

'I'll run to the IGA,' I say.

'Been there already this morning – they didn't have any left,' Seth tells me.

Alejandra is looking in the fridge – not much chance of getting lost in there.

'Hey, you little idiot,' the guy calls out; I *think* he means Seth but I'm not feeling too clever either, 'cream!'

Seth is shaking, I'll be there soon, but Alejandra seems calm.

'Let me help,' she says, pulling a can of whipped cream from the fridge. She charges out of the kitchen whilst shaking the can furiously before we have a chance to question her plan.

Seth and I watch as she lashes the lacking nachos with a blizzard of the sugary dairy substitute.

'Enjoy!' Alejandra tells the red face.

I immediately calm the guy down with a refund while I encourage Alejandra to rejoin the crew out front. Seth, meanwhile, looks energised and merrily sorts out the kitchen, which is now most definitely closed for lunch.

■ ■ ■

Enough people file in as to require me to stay behind the bar, but Andrew doesn't make a reappearance inside so the register is running low on coins. I'm not likely to call Logan though.

'Alejandra's cool,' Seth tells me.

'She's never dull,' I say.

'I can watch the bar if you like.'

'Cheers.'

Just as I sit down, interrupting Andrew recounting his tales of woe to Alejandra, a cab pulls up. It's Travis.

I feel like I'm on the receiving end of an episode of *This Is Your Life*. Is my father in the green room?

Travis sees us, waves and starts to walk over, pulling his airline stewards' bag – no doubt full of free designer clothes.

After tripping over the kerb he joins us, saying, 'We had a shoot at an abandoned warehouse not far from here – *industrial chic* apparently – so I thought I'd swing by.'

The old lady wakes up when Travis knocks into the table and she pats his bag on the head. 'Nice doggie.'

'This is my *old* friend Andrew,' Alejandra says to Travis.

'Oh,' Travis replies, shaking Andrew's knight-free hand. 'How long have you known each other?'

'About two hours,' Alejandra says.

Once the chess game is won by Andrew, both he and the other guy announce they're both exhausted and can't do another jug. Who's going to be the last men slumping now? We're going to have to lay off staff – if we had any.

'I'm stuffed – I'm going home to sleep. Nice to meet you both,' Andrew says to Alejandra and Travis, then, 'See ya Ethan.'

'See ya.'

After the other guy has left, and the old lady is busy talking to Travis's bag, Alejandra says to me, 'I think all that turkey is putting them to sleep.'

'Think so?'

'Yeah, I do,' she says, smiling *that* smile of hers.

'What are you up to this evening?' I ask Travis, who seems to be editing the databank of names in his phone. From what I can tell he adds and deletes on a daily basis.

'Undecided as yet – I'm waiting to hear back from Zac. Hey, speaking of which, are you both coming to my birthday drinks?'

'Sure,' I say, waiting to be dittoed. Please ditto me.

'*¿Porqué no?*' Alejandra says.

'They serve tapas there if you want to eat,' Travis says.

I'm sure Alejandra *wants* to eat, if she will is another matter.

'Don't know what shirt I'm going to wear to cover tapas,' Travis muses.

'Why don't you just wear black?' Alejandra asks. 'That covers all.'

Travis considers this, then, looking embarrassed, says, 'Why didn't I think of that? Man, I can be an idiot.'

'You know what?' Alejandra says. 'I reckon it's *smart* to add colour to things Travis.'

Travis appears chuffed by this endorsement, in contrast to the blank expressions I've seen him offer when someone salivates over his looks. He checks his phone again but it's got nothing to report.

'Show me how this thing works,' I say to Travis, who has set his phone back down.

'You just scroll through the list like this.'

'What if you want to jump to a number – say Zac's for example,' I ask.

'Here you go – Zac's number.' Travis shows me how quickly you can pull up one person out of hundreds.

I head back inside to check Seth is okay and within minutes Logan arrives via the front.

'That daft old bird outside just introduced me to someone very interesting,' Logan says to me.

'Oh, who?' I stammer.

'Apparently there's a bag out there pretending to be a dog, pretending to be a certain Travis Lever – your old boss from Baxter's.'

23. More is Less

Just as I'm getting off the phone Alejandra arrives.

'Who was that?' she asks.

'Nobody.'

'How *is* nobody? I've been meaning to give them a call myself.'

'It was just this guy Zac – a friend of Travis's.'

'This place is pretty chilled,' Alejandra says, surveying the intimate bar that Travis chose to birthday drink in.

I take another look around. Taking up the ground level of a terrace on Little Lonsdale Street there is basically one space at the front, where the bar and a bunch of tables are, and then a few steps down to another space where Alejandra and I have claimed one of the sofas. At the very back is a raised level that could squeeze in a three-member band, four if they're tight, but is currently occupied by a pool table. The entire place has cool lighting, floorboards and mismatched furniture. It feels more like a home than a nightspot.

'So, what's on the menu?' Alejandra asks.

'Here you go,' I say, passing her the modest food listing I collected from the bar when I arrived.

'I meant – who can I expect to meet tonight?' she says, casually glancing at the menu.

'I've only met a few of Travis's friends,' I tell her. 'There's his bestie Zac, and Siimon – who works in the fashion industry, two "i"s apparently, but he likes to be called the Silver Fox. I've also met Tatiana – another model.'

Alejandra looks at the present on the small table in front of us.

'Nice wrapping, Ethan. I like the serrated edge and how you endeavoured to make the tape stretch over the shortfall in paper.'

Travis's gift has seen me finally use up the roll of all-purpose wrap that had lasted me close on a decade. It gave me a sense of achievement.

'Thanks for coming along,' I say to Alejandra.

'No worries.'

I get us a couple of beers and we talk about Alejandra's first week at Tate Lane – nice enough place, glee-club colleagues, nut-job boss, wanker authors – and my week of looking for work again since Logan told me to split. He didn't take the whole Travis-being-my-previous-boss scam that well.

'So, any possibilities?' Alejandra asks me.

'I actually rang this friend of my dad's who works in television. She gave me her card a while back.'

'And?'

'She told me they need someone temporarily on the set she's currently working on – mundane gopher stuff, I assume. Should do me for a week or so.'

'If you last,' Alejandra ribs me.

'If I last.'

Travis arrives next, with a girl I've not seen before.

'This is Sonia,' Travis says.

Sonia has green eyes, a cute trail of freckles across her nose and long chestnut hair.

'We met on the tram,' Sonia announces.

'You're having the meatballs I assume?' Alejandra says to Travis, eyeing his tomato-coloured shirt.

'They're fantastic,' Travis replies.

'Are all your shirts from the warmer side of the colour spectrum?'

'There aren't many blue foods,' Travis says.

'Quite right,' Alejandra says.

Sonia looks a little confused.

'I like to coordinate,' Travis explains.

This is where Zac would take a cheap shot, but he's not here yet.

Whilst Travis is getting drinks Sonia tells us about how hot Travis is.

'Couldn't you just eat him up,' she announces breathlessly, looking at both Alejandra *and* me.

'He's my stepbrother,' I say flatly.

'And I'm not that hungry,' Alejandra says.

'I felt a real connection to him – as soon as I spotted him. And then when he sat next to me I knew he must have felt it too.'

'Was the tram crowded?' Alejandra asks.

Sonia ignores the question and continues on about the kismet of their meeting.

'That's really beautiful,' Alejandra says and I suppress a smile.

'Isn't he though?' Sonia says.

Travis returns but Sonia continues unabated.

'I love your hair. Oh, and your eyes. I can't choose my favourite – your blond hair or your blue eyes. What's *your* favourite?' Sonia asks Travis.

Travis squirms visibly and I think he's already wishing he'd left this present unwrapped and lonely on the tram.

'Come on – what's your favourite part of your look, Travis?' Sonia repeats the question.

'I'm happy having eyes,' Travis says. 'How's that?'

'No, I mean …'

'We saw the sweetest thing on the tram,' Travis starts, swiftly changing the focus. 'There was this genteel-looking old lady – must have been about eighty – and she had a guide dog. She was sat opposite us and this young guy gets on and sits next to her. He was the roughest-looking dude you've ever seen – covered in tats and piercings, the lot. Anyway, the blind granny starts talking to him and by the time we get off they're chatting away about the weather and dogs and all sorts.'

Meanwhile, from her expression, Sonia seems to remember the same story with horror.

'It was so cool,' Travis says.

'It was *so* disturbing,' Sonia says, 'Someone should have saved her.'

Travis is looking at his phone.

'Tatiana can't make it.'

Up at the bar I can see Zac and Siimon. Travis spots them as well.

'Ha! Ethan – I bet you thought Zac wouldn't show!' Travis says proudly.

'Here he is,' I say.

Zac walks towards us as if he were being filmed.

'*Happening* place,' Zac says sarcastically, handing a T-shirt in a plastic bag to Travis. 'Happy Birthday.'

Travis pulls the T-shirt out of the bag – it says, *Quality frames don't guarantee quality pictures*.

Siimon claims his share of the credit: 'We saw it on our way here and I thought of you.'

Travis thanks them both and I just look at Alejandra. Am I being oversensitive? She seems to think they're taking a shot as well.

Travis starts on the introductions.

'Alejandra, Sonia, this is Siimon – with two "i"s.'

'Oh, I've heard about you,' Alejandra says. 'The Grey Fox.'

'That's *Silver* Fox,' Siimon snaps back.

'And this is Zac,' Travis says.

'First Travis, now you!' Sonia drools. 'You two are hot.'

Cheers Sonia.

'Well, that's why they pay us the big bucks,' Zac says, in the same tone as if to say, *Duh!*

'You're a model?' Sonia turns on Travis. 'You never said!'

'Um, sorry,' Travis says, setting to replace his crisp red shirt with the cryptic white T-shirt. 'I guess.'

'My friends are going to die!' Sonia screams and then dies a little herself when Travis is mid shirt change.

'I think I recognise you now,' Sonia says, slobbering a little. Zac thinks she's referring to him.

'*You're* the Diesel guy,' Sonia says to Travis. 'From the billboards.'

'That campaign is *over*,' Zac tells Sonia. 'Move on.'

'So what's it like, Travis?' Sonia gushes. 'Being a model?'

'It's okay,' he says. 'Lots of walking.'

'Walking is instinctual for those in our profession,' Zac proclaims. 'You have it or you *just don't*. That's what makes models special – instinct.'

'All living things have instincts – so not that special,' Alejandra says.

'Oh really,' Zac stares Alejandra down, 'what about a ... um, say a banana – what instinct does it have?'

'It knows to go bad as soon as you've left the supermarket with it,' Alejandra replies.

Sonia, sitting on the other side of Alejandra, turns to her and asks, 'Do you watch *America's Next Top Model*?'

Alejandra is really straining not to be overtly rude to any of Travis's guests. I feel like I'm watching the tide being held back just before a tsunami hits.

'I don't usually watch reality television,' Alejandra says. 'It's not what I'd hope real people would be like.'

Alejandra is no use as a springboard for Sonia so she zones in again on her preferred demographic.

'I'm thinking of changing my "i" to a "y" actually,' Sonia, or possibly Sonya, says to the hot guys.

'Why?' Travis asks.

'Well, Siiiiiimon can't take the discarded vowel,' Alejandra says to me, a little too loudly. 'He has more than enough "i"s already.'

I resort to an old standard to help divert attention,

'So, Sonia, where are you from?'

'South Melbourne,' Sonia replies, and then somewhat proudly, 'home of the dim sim!'

Alejandra surprisingly resists that and Sonia adds, 'You guys?'

'North,' Alejandra says.

'I'm sorry?' Sonia has just noticed Siimon's ironed-on quizzical expression.

'I didn't say anything,' Siimon tells her.

'Garth says Happy Birthday but can't make it,' Travis reads from his phone.

Sonia looks a little lost so continues with stretching the geography discussion.

'What about you Ethan – where do you hang?'

'I tend to stick to the city,' I say.

'Like a pigeon,' Alejandra says, which allows us both to laugh at the past half-hour's conversation under the guise of this last comment.

Travis cajoles Zac, Siimon and Sonia into playing doubles on the pool table. Apparently the winners will play me and Alejandra, but that won't be happening soon given their immediate poor form.

'We have to get Travis to take that stupid T-shirt off,' I say to Alejandra. 'And not for Sonia's benefit.'

'Look at you being all defensive of your stepbro,' Alejandra says.

'It's just that –'

'It's nice to see you worked up over something,' Alejandra cuts me off.

After Travis suspends play so he can head to the bar to get drinks for everyone, Zac and Sonia pass the time giggling about some guy nearby – sitting alone. They seem sure they have something the guy doesn't have – I can't tell you what that is though. An hour ago Sonia was by herself on a tram, but that irony would be lost on her.

Travis drops off two beers for me and Alejandra.

'Here's your present, buddy.' I pass the gift over carefully, so the wrapping won't disintegrate before he opens it.

'Cheers Ethan,' Travis says, opening the gift. 'Another T-shirt – thanks mate!'

'No worries,' I say.

We pass on the opportunity to challenge the winners, so the others play a second game and I get to enjoy Alejandra's company some more. Her stories from just a week at her new job keep me laughing through several beers.

'Beer, Dopey?' I hear Zac ask Travis, and on his way to the bar he calls by our table.

'Do you guys want anything?'

'No thanks,' we both reply automatically.

'You should be buying me a round, Ethan,' Zac tells me.

'Why's that?' Alejandra asks.

'Ethan called and *demanded* I come tonight,' Zac says before heading to the bar.

Alejandra looks at me and, briefly brushing her hand against mine, says with a smile, 'So you're to blame for that idiot.'

'Travis likes him,' I say.

On his way back Zac stops again and asks, 'Are you guys going out tonight?'

What the fuck? This is it. This *is* going out tonight.

'We're staying here,' Alejandra replies.

Zac surveys the uncrowded place. 'This joint is a bit like Travis – the lights are on but no one's home.'

I think about my old, empty house with blazing lights. And I think about Travis.

'Just joking,' Zac says, aware from my face that I'm not laughing.

'Well, it ain't funny,' I tell Zac. 'It's time you laid off the Travis jokes.'

'Whatever,' Zac says before walking back to the pool table.

Within minutes everybody is back at the table.

'So are you coming or not?' Zac asks Travis. 'I can *probably* get you in if you want.'

'I'm going to stay,' Travis says.

'Okay,' Zac says and prepares to leave with Siimon. And Sonia it seems.

The three of them offer limp farewells. Sonia seems torn but Travis is making no overtures so she gets drawn to the other magnet.

'Nice to meet you Siiiiiimon, Son-yah,' Alejandra says a little too close to earshot, 'and Zoolander.'

When they've gone Travis sits down, apparently relieved.

'So Travis,' Alejandra says, 'do you think you've found her – your one true soulless mate?'

Travis laughs. He's still wearing Zac and Siimon's gift, which I swear is intended to take the piss out of him when they're not around to do it themselves.

'You should put on the T-shirt Ethan gave you,' Alejandra tells Travis.

'After I've eaten,' Travis replies.

Tugging at the Zac shirt he adds, 'This one will be perfect to mop up spills.'

24. The Collectors

It may be a coincidence but shortly after Zac and his wing-cretins leave, the place fills up. Smart crowd.

The three of us are restricted space-wise now that the place is pumping: a single sofa and two jugs of beer between us – we are well settled in.

'Thanks for coming, guys,' Travis says to us both as he finishes off his meatballs soaked in radioactive-red sauce.

'I wouldn't have missed out on Sonia-time for all the world,' Alejandra, stuck between me and Travis, says.

'That reminds me – I should delete her from my phone,' Travis says. His address book is more alive than Mister Fantastic.

'You should never put someone into your phone on first meeting,' Alejandra notes. 'It's like sleeping with someone on the first date.'

'I'll remember that,' Travis replies, then asks, 'Ethan, do you ever cull people?'

'I'm still very much in collecting mode,' I answer.

Travis muses. 'Maybe the big gang theory – more friends the better – is overrated.'

'I've got a ways to go before that's my problem,' I reply.

Travis's phone requests attention again. We listen in to his side of a polite but vague conversation. I refuel our glasses – hopefully neither Alejandra nor Travis decides this is lame and decides to head home soon. This is as good a home as I can imagine right now.

'Okay, thanks for the call – nice to hear from you.'

'Who was that?' Alejandra asks Travis.

Travis looks at his phone. 'I don't know.'

'That was a mighty long conversation for a wrong number,' Alejandra says, easing her confusion with a mighty slug of beer. Like a model she seems concerned only with calories that come with chewing.

'I don't know her name,' Travis explains. 'From what I could tell she was a lady I met I when collected for charity.'

'That reminds me actually.' I say to Travis. 'When I worked at the call centre …'

'For a day,' Alejandra interjects.

'… for a day, there was a lady there who remembered you from when you called on her place for the Red Cross …'

'Huh,' Travis says, seemingly bored.

'… and I recall, another time, seeing a different lady hanging outside your house waiting for you.'

I leave off the *A-ha!*

Travis looks like he's about to say something, stops himself and pours some beer down his throat – both inside and out – instead.

'Spill it,' Alejandra says and we all laugh.

'You'll think I'm a real jerk,' Travis says.

'Too late,' Alejandra replies with a smile.

'I'd been pretty mediocre at my previous jobs and I wanted to be the best charity collector they had …'

'Yeeesss,' Alejandra hurries him along so he can't edit too much out whilst thinking out loud.

'… so, anyway, I became the best collector they had. And it *was* for a very good cause. And no commission. That's important to note – no commission!' Travis says.

'I don't get it,' I say.

'Travis came for charity,' Alejandra tells me.

'Okay – before you both get the wrong impression entirely,' Travis says, 'I always checked they weren't married …'

'They could have removed their ring,' Alejandra says.

'Then it would be *them* who were cheating.'

'Fair enough,' Alejandra concedes.

'How did you bring it up – so to speak – I mean, how did you let them know what was on offer?'

'If she was watching the W Channel in trakky daks, eating a Lean Cuisine and petting a cat then it was a wink and straight into it,' Alejandra says, laughing.

'It was just a look and they would make an awfully large contribution and one thing would lead to another,' Travis clarifies.

'And everyone was happy,' Alejandra says, raising her empty glass.

'I got a plaque,' Travis says.

'Your teeth look fine to me,' Alejandra says.

'I'm getting more beer,' Travis smiles, and I notice he is blushing, which is strangely reassuring.

The crowd has moved on again. It's like this bar is some craggy rock on the very tip of the Cape of Good Hope – momentarily overwhelmed by migrating hordes and quickly emptied again as the wind changes.

Travis returns with another jug *and* an old guy who looks like part of the furniture.

'This is Oscar,' Travis introduces the friendly-looking man. 'He owns this place. Oscar – this is my brother Ethan, and this is Alejandra.'

I like it when Travis removes the *step*.

'Have you had a good night?' Oscar asks us both.

'Yeah,' I say. 'It's a great little place.'

'We have been very happy here for nearly thirty years,' Oscar says nostalgically.

'Do you live here as well?' Alejandra asks. She looks as relaxed as I can remember and has seemingly forgotten she's addicted to nicotine.

'There's a flat upstairs,' Oscar tells us. 'My daughters grew up with all the life and noise below to fall asleep to. They reckon they miss it now.'

I can understand that.

'What is this place called?' Travis asks. 'I've only ever know the address.'

'Officially it's simply called Oscar's, but there's no name out front,' Oscar says. 'We wanted people to refer to it as the place with no name – adds a little mystery.'

'That's cool,' Travis says. 'If I had a bar I'd call it the Bar.'

Not for the first time tonight Alejandra holds her tongue.

'So,' Travis explains, 'when people say "Let's go to the bar" my place would be front of mind.'

'Not bad,' Oscar says.

'At all,' Alejandra adds.

'Do you have any plans for the place?' I ask Oscar.

'Actually me and my wife can sense the warmer weather up north calling us,' Oscar replies. 'Maybe we'll go this year or next – when the timing is right.'

'Speaking of which – is it closing time already?' Travis asks politely, noticing that we have the place pretty much to ourselves.

'Stay as long as you like,' Oscar replies, and leaves us to finish our jug.

'I think Joy would like this place,' Travis says.

'That reminds me,' I say. 'We should continue showing her more of Japan.'

'So, what's next on the going-Japanese-in-Melbourne agenda?' Alejandra asks.

'I'll make a plan,' I say.

The best part of this entire night is now. Just the three of us remain, none of us going anywhere, and it feels complete.

25. On 'Can't' Alert

'We couldn't convince Jake Gyllenhaal,' Kate tells me sadly.

'Yeah, but Josh Hartnett – that's still pretty cool,' I say.

Kate, my father's friend and film industry colleague, is about to run me through the drill for my temporary stint – doing anything that no one else wants to do – on the set of *Ganglands 3*. Apparently they're doing all the scenes that feature the character of Wayne, heroic young constable, as quickly as possible. They've only got Josh Hartnett's attention for a week.

'The producers reckon they'll be able to sell the series to the US on the back of a name actor being involved.'

'So what specifically do I do?' I ask.

'Well, you'll come along with us to the different locations where scenes featuring Josh – *Wayne* – are filmed. His minders are all Americans, but we need an Australian along to assist as well.'

'How come?'

'Now as I recall, Ethan,' Kate says, 'when you were a kid – whenever we'd come to party at your dad's place – you had a very observant nature. Didn't you memorise all our car numberplates?'

'Yeah, I liked visitors coming over.'

'Really?' Kate says. 'You didn't actually speak that much to any of us.'

'I just liked people in the house.'

'Anyway,' Kate continues, 'we need to harness your skills.'

Not something I hear often.

'You may know that we employ a method of semi-improvisation – the scripts are relatively fluid so as to keep things fresh and spontaneous. The focus is on the characters themselves,' Kate explains.

'Okay.'

'Some people are not built for spontaneity,' Kate says. 'You know what I mean, Ethan?'

'Sure do.'

'The character is Australian and our accent is a challenge for any foreign actor, but Josh thinks he's going to be Meryl Streep. What you have to do is be his shadow and solely focus on picking up any instances where he mispronounces a word. Everyone else on set will be distracted by their own roles and chores, so we need someone as our trained set of ears.'

'I can listen,' I say.

'It'll be too late or awkward to fix up any slip-throughs in editing as Josh will be long gone – we need to redo any mistakes immediately. You'll be our wicket keeper.'

I nod that I get her sporting analogy – which I guess she's thrown into the mix since I'm a guy.

'Is that challenging enough for you, Ethan? We can't use someone who bores easily and simply wants to move up to more complex tasks.'

'Perfect.'

'Now, tomatoes and bananas anyone can catch,' Kate tells me. 'We need a more subtle ear. With improv the actors may slip in *can't* or *sure* before you know where you are.'

'Is there a list of words I need to listen out for?' I ask.

'We can make one on our way to the first location.'

As we walk through the carpark of the production offices I ask Kate if she has the same car.

'Yes – it's ancient now.'

'ESD-511.'

'The job's yours!' Kate says.

'So where are we shooting first?' I say, fully on board with the industry lingo now.

'A restaurant in Seddon – Wayne is secretly meeting a Vietnamese girl whose brothers are members of a triad.'

Kate hands me a pad of post-its and a pen and we brainstorm words to listen out for as we drive out to the burbs.

'So, we have tomato, banana, can't, sure ...' Kate dictates.

'Laugh,' I say, writing it down.

'Yes,' Kate says.

'Yes?'

'No, I mean *laugh* is a yes,' Kate replies, laughing. Or is it laffing?

'Fast and last.' I add to them to the list.

Kate has quit commending me for fear I'll write down everything she says.

'You must have had lots of parties when you were a kid, what with having the house to yourself so much,' Kate muses.

'It seemed smarter to keep the empty-place thing to myself.'

'Rather.'

I look at her in confusion.

'*Rather*. That's another one – write it down,' Kate says.

'Shur will,' I say, smiling.

'I bet you miss your dad, I know I do.'

'Yeah,' I say.

'He'd be chuffed that you're working on set.'

I grin and it takes a few beats to lose it.

'Pass, fragile, duty, ask,' Kate says.

I try to imagine the cast of *Friends*. What might they say?

'Aunt, half, after, semi ...'

■ ■ ■

'Ethan, this is Josh.'

'Wayne,' Josh says.

He's in character apparently.

'Hey,' I say and shake his hand.

'And this is Alice. In this scene Alice is covertly meeting Wayne in this out-of-the-way restaurant.'

'Alice,' Alice says.

'Is that your real name or your character's name?' I ask.

'Both.'

The director's assistant, who Kate awarded me to when we arrived on set, reminds me that my only assignment is to listen to every word out of Josh Hartnett's mouth. Like a groupie might. I won't be alone, it seems – the makeup girls and more than one of the techies are also hanging around the American star like so much driftwood.

Josh takes a final look at the script and Alice takes her seat at a table in the back of the restaurant that's full of extras preparing to linger over their cold-looking meals whilst holding fake, mumbled conversations with each other.

'Action.'

Josh enters the restaurant, removes his shades and cases the place for anyone watching him – which, ironically, everybody is – but as Wayne he fails to notice this. He joins Alice at her discreetly positioned table whilst I ensure that I remain just out of shot but within earshot.

Wayne: 'Did you come alone?'

That sounds Australian to me.

Alice: 'Of course. Do you think I'm stupid?'

I prepare for Josh to use the word 'stupid' back at her. I'm sweating on it.

Wayne: 'Usually girls who look as good as you are – just a little.'

Oh crap – and speaking of stupid …

Alice: 'Should I be insulted?'

She's flirting with him. I wonder if that's in the script.

Wayne: 'Not at all. Now tell me, Alice, what's new with your family?'

He said *noo*! I'm ecstatic. I wave at the director's assistant and ...

'Cut.'

Before they recommence, the director's assistant comes over to me.

'Good pick-up Ethan.'

'Thanks.'

'Ethan, we're actually short an extra – how would you like to help out?'

'Um. Okay,' I say.

'Great. What you're wearing is perfect for the role. We just need you to come off the street – you stagger through the restaurant, knocking into tables, searching for some guy called Gavin. You're probably stoned. Make your way through the place, finally crashing into Wayne and Alice's table, which causes Alice to drop her bag and a handgun falls out.'

'Easy peasy,' I say.

'Japanesey,' she replies instantly, before adding the warning, 'You still have to keep an eye, I mean ear, out for Josh, I mean Wayne.'

The director's assistant lets me look at the relevant script page but all I have to say is the one word over and over – *Gavin*. It's more of an action role. I'm assured that I won't need to join equity even though it is, strictly speaking, a talking part. At second glance I see that my character's name is Flunky in Restaurant.

Flunky in Restaurant: 'Gavin?'

Flunky in Restaurant crashes into tables, haranguing patrons, until reaching the table in back.

Flunky in Restaurant: 'Gavin? Where's Gavin?'

I improvised the *Where's*.

Wayne: *Standing Up.* 'There's no Gavin here mate. Fuck off.'

Flunky in Restaurant crashes into Wayne's table, Alice's bag drops to floor, handgun falls out. Flunky in Restaurant leaves, calling out 'Gavin' all the while.

■ ■ ■

Apparently I did a stand-up job with the acting – unfortunately, however, in the midst of the commotion, Wayne improvised, referring to Flunky in Restaurant knocking over the table's *vaze* and I wasn't there to catch it.

26. Street Walkers

'How many versions of your résumé do you have there?'

I flip through the wad of one-pagers. 'Just one version – the super-generic rendition of my last decade.'

To cover the lack of actual achievements I packed it with aspirations and some other shit that prospective employers seem addicted to.

Alejandra pulls me in under her umbrella so my résumé won't get wetter.

'Thanks for taking the day off,' I say again.

'I consider it a twenty-four-hour advance on my weekend,' Alejandra tells me.

Normally when I know I'll be entering shops I purposely dress down so as to ensure I'm not bothered by anyone. But today I'm trying to impress – and not just the vendors.

'You look employable,' Alejandra tells me.

'Cheers,' I say.

I point out the Sushi Train where I've already left my résumé once before. The sign, seeking a cashier/attendant who speaks English, remains in the window however.

'In you go,' Alejandra says.

Walking past the giant Scaletrix race track where salmon and tuna are plying through their laps, I make my way toward the chef at the far end of the restaurant.

'Hi, I left my résumé here a couple of weeks back but have not heard anything,' I say as unnarkily as possible. 'Can I leave this with you again to pass on for me?'

I wave my résumé at him and he nods that he'll concede to doing this.

'Thanks,' I say animatedly, under the ridiculous notion that come the time he gives my résumé to whoever's in charge he'll recall this exuberance and be driven to be my advocate.

The next place that has a 'seeking staff' sign in the window has an additional sign promoting the availability of *fresh* milkshakes.

'Maybe not,' Alejandra says.

Ahead of us a uni-student type drops a scrap of notepaper on the ground. Alejandra calls after him,

'Excuse me. You dropped something.'

Alejandra points at the piece of paper. Rain has clocked off for the moment and wind is commencing its shift so the discarded paper is on the move.

'Oh, thanks,' he says cheerily, before assuring her, 'It's just rubbish.'

'Yeah I know,' Alejandra tells him. 'You dropped it on the street. There are bins everywhere.'

'Oh, okay.'

Alejandra says to me, 'When I was a little kid littering was *the* environmental issue.'

'Look at that,' I say, pointing out a shop window that features new toasters – quite slick looking ones – for $3.95 each. 'It weirds me out for some reason.'

'To think not so long ago people used to give those as wedding gifts,' Alejandra says. 'I feel so old.'

Cartridge World has a notice: *Highly motivated salesperson required* ...

'I don't think I want to spend forty hours a week with someone so fucked up that the thought of flogging cartridges finds them *highly motivated.'*

'You're not alone,' Alejandra assures me.

■ ■ ■

Mostly we just leave résumés followed by smile chasers before legging it, but occasionally they want to assess you on the spot. Cafés seem the most desperate.

'Are you confident about working in food?' Alejandra asks me as we stand outside the Blue Moose Café.

'I'm discovering that getting the job is the most difficult part,' I tell Alejandra. 'The boss will always make out it's all so challenging, but once you get in the door they're no longer around and the mentor they've assigned you is mostly all about doing everything themself.'

'I like your confidence,' Alejandra says.

On returning to the street I tell Alejandra,'They had me dice an onion.'

'Not so good?'

'Not so good.'

I put my bleeding finger inside my pocket.

■ ■ ■

The sun is working the afternoon grind – today's weather has changed more often than Travis during Fashion Week – and recharges my enthusiasm. I even go into a kebab place – late nights shaving meat for trainee alcoholics would certainly introduce me to a whole new cast of characters – and wait at the counter. The guy wielding the knife turns on the spot slowly – like a lamb spire.

'G'day mate,' he says.

'I was wondering if you have any work going.'

'Not at the moment, my friend.'

'Okay,' I say. 'Two chicken kebabs please.'

'The lot?'

'The lot.'

Me and Alejandra sit on the grass outside the state library and I eat one and a half chicken kebabs.

'So tell me more about things at Tate Lane,' I ask Alejandra.

'It's fine.'

'More!' I demand.

'Well, I immediately got assigned to looking after the final stages of pushing the latest book from our local star author through production,' Alejandra says. 'That's been no fun.'

'Why?'

'T.C. Bryce, the author, doesn't suffer fools …'

'You're no fool,' I say.

'Thanks Ethan, but to him I'm barely literate.'

'Does he make you look stupid?' I ask, as if that were even possible.

'He makes himself look stupid, though I'm probably the only one at Tate Lane who sees it that way,' Alejandra says. 'Oh, and he calls me *Sandra*!'

'Do you remind him of your real name?'

'That makes him more defiant, it seems.'

'Fuck him over then.'

'I'll try,' she says with a smile.

Pointing out a guy in a suit running desperately to catch the 16 tram before it takes off, Alejandra says, 'Do you want him to make it?'

'Yes,' I say automatically, and then ask her, 'Don't you?'

'I suppose – I'd just rather he didn't run after it in the first place.'

■ ■ ■

At Mooks, the lethargic cashier, kept upright by a luminescent sports drink, refers us to the manager who is walking the floor. She looks at my résumé briefly before stating, 'We want somebody with that special something.'

I turn out my pockets and Alejandra laughs too loudly.

■ ■ ■

By day's end I've hacked away at four onions. The Blue Moose said, 'I think your finger's bleeding'; the Fat Yak was surprised that I'd left it so late to remove the peel; the Dancing Goat told me sarcastically that, 'At this rate you'll get through, what, half-a-dozen onions a shift'; and the Three Buffalos declared my wedges 'too Asian'. The Arrogant Frog and the Lazy Duck weren't looking for anyone. I never came upon a Silver Fox though.

■ ■ ■

'So you actually met Josh Hartnett?' Travis asks immediately prior to getting egg on his face.

'Sure did,' I say, smiling like a wanker. 'He's nice people.'

'Loser,' Alejandra says.

'No, he's not!' I protest with a grin.

'You, I mean.'

The rest of us successfully manage to catch the egg being flung around by our teppanyaki cook.

'And you'll actually appear in *Ganglands 3*?' Joy asks me as prawns hit the hotplate we're positioned around. The four of us are sharing the food thrower with a good-looking couple and two older women who flinch each time the cook looks their way.

'If they don't cut me,' I reply. 'I had a line to say – so I'll be in the credits.'

'What was your name?' Travis asks me.

'I played the part of Flunky in Restaurant.'

'Huh?' Travis says.

'I knock over a table and spill stuff.'

'Guess that makes me a flunky too,' Travis says before mistiming his catch and getting a prawn's head caught in his long hair.

'How did you go today?' Joy asks me, quietly evading food and hoping we'll not notice. She looks tired but insisted we not can the night, saying this trip to Southgate, in Alejandra's car, would brighten her up no end.

'We went into heaps of places,' I tell Joy.

'And massacred a field's worth of onions,' Alejandra chimes in.

'Cafés seem to favour deducing kitchen skills by having you dice an onion,' I explain.

'And?' Joy asks.

'I failed.'

'I've suggested Ethan come over to my place tomorrow for some onion training before he tries a particularly cool-looking café on Little Bourke we spotted,' Alejandra tells Joy.

The attractive couple – Brad and Angelina – is having a lot of sake-inspired fun. Originally I'd presumed they were married but now I'm not so sure. The older ladies, meanwhile, are eating even less than Joy – determined as they are to avoid eye contact with the cook and his errant spatulas.

'Have you ever had teppanyaki before?' Alejandra asks Joy.

'No. I've always wanted to,' Joy says. 'Markus told me once how much he enjoyed it.'

Alejandra looks at me but I've no more to add – that's news to me as well.

'Sounds like you had a lot in common,' Alejandra says to Joy, before remembering that they met through both having the same terminal disease. Alejandra looks mortified.

'I'm sorry – that was really thoughtless of me.' She looks like she's going to cry.

'Don't be silly, sweetie,' Joy tells Alejandra. 'Several times Markus and I talked about how much we had in common – not least each of us having a single child who was the most important thing in our world.'

Shit – now *I'm* going to cry. I look over at Travis but he has been momentarily distracted by Angelina. With Brad having darted off to take a call on his mobile, Angelina leans over and passes Travis her card.

'Wow,' I whisper to Travis, who tears the card in half and then drowns it in his finger bowl for good measure.

Alejandra and Joy are oblivious to all this and I hear Joy telling Alejandra how bad my father felt about leaving me with no family. I'm learning heaps being sat in the middle.

Travis and I eat the flesh of at least six different animal types while Alejandra and Joy discuss more life-affirming topics than Oprah knew existed. Once we've paid and are setting to leave, Brad scrawls something on a scrap of paper and brazenly offers it to Travis.

Waving off the number Travis says simply, 'I'm with my family.'

■ ■ ■

On the way back through the city Joy asks Alejandra if she wouldn't mind driving past the bar we had Travis's birthday drinks at. Alejandra, driving with straight arms that make it appear she's attempting to push the steering wheel through the windscreen, is up for the diversion. Joy turns around with the fragility of someone twice her age.

'You three had a great night, I understand,' she says before quickly turning back.

'So much fun that I forgot to jerk off when I got home,' Travis tells me quietly.

I laugh, and whisper back, 'Or maybe you were just too drunk.'

'That might also have been a contributing factor to the negligence of my regular routine,' Travis concedes.

Alejandra pauses outside the unlabelled bar and relaxes her arms for a bit. Joy scrutinises the facade, conceding the place does indeed look real cosy, before we continue on to North Melbourne – aka Our Little Tokyo.

'Let's drink some Kirin beer and watch cable,' Travis suggests.

'We can laugh at Fox News,' Alejandra says.

'Forget that – I've got us a DVD and some Japanese candy,' I say, holding up the plastic bag I've been carrying all night.

'I was wondering what you had there,' Joy says. 'I thought you might have been moving house.'

'What's the movie?' Travis asks.

'*Godzilla*,' I announce proudly.

■ ■ ■

Showtime is running with *The Butterfly Effect* so we watch Ashton Kutcher busily acting away for a bit until everyone is settled in.

'Oh, pause for a moment, Ethan, will you?' Joy asks.

'It's not playing yet,' I say.

'I've got something for Alejandra.'

Joy steps over me and Travis before searching in the kitchen for a moment. She returns to the sofa and presents Alejandra with a mortar and pestle.

'I want you to have this,' Joy says as Alejandra protests in vain.

We all go quiet as Alejandra finally concedes to accepting the gift and all it implies.

'Candy!' Travis calls out.

I support this attempt at distraction and spill the bag's contents onto the floor.

'Okay, we have: Walky Walky candy pellets – I think you shake a load in your mouth and pass the cup on; cola-flavoured Pokemon-shaped lollipops encased in bags of "sizzling" powder; Happy Strawberry Crunky – strawberry-flavoured white chocolate; and finally Black Black Gum.'

'Eek – what's Black Black Gum?' Alejandra asks, implying the other items pass muster.

I read from the pack. 'It says here *Promises Hi-Technical Excellent Taste and Flavour.*'

We charge ourselves with sugar. Alejandra asks Travis to put on the subtitles as his crunching is too loud. Diego joins us and chooses to sleep on Joy. The radiated lizard finds its way to America – so we cheer for the monster. By the end a single Godzilla egg has survived the mayhem and we are happy.

'I'm exhausted,' Joy says.

'We should leave,' I say.

'The good exhausted,' Joy responds and kisses each of us goodnight. 'Stay so I can fall asleep listening to you.'

27. The Onion Test

'Which colour?'

'It doesn't matter, Ethan, they're all onions,' Alejandra says, placing a cutting board on her kitchen bench. 'Select your favourite.'

'So, basically, they're all the same?'

My hand wavers over the bowl of onions that mix in complete harmony.

'If you cut an onion will you not cry?' Alejandra says.

I choose one and set it on the board. The sun streams through the kitchen window with each sway of the leaf-ladened tree outside. Momentarily the onion is lit up as if it's just walked on stage. To face execution.

'I like your place,' I tell Alejandra – which allows me a free pass to gawk a bit more.

'Thanks.'

I glance again at the fridge and Alejandra is finally compelled to explain the particular formation created by the colourful magnetic letters.

'Damien spelt it out for me.'

'Do you think four exclamation points was a little overkill?'

'He's very passionate about *that* topic.'

I really don't like to hear the words 'Damien' and 'passionate' in the same sentence. But now I have a new word to hate: *'Treadmill!!!!'*

'Okay Ethan,' Alejandra distracts me from commenting, 'first you cut the onion in half – lengthways from bulb end to tip.'

Alejandra expertly makes a considered and unfussy single action.

'Remove the skin like this – leaving the bulb intact.'

This is already different to each of my previous attempts at winging this skill.

'Then, using the tip of the knife, cut the onion lengthways into even slices, leaving – this is important Ethan,' Alejandra stresses, 'leaving the slices attached to the bulb.'

Who'd have thought something so simple could be so complicated?

'Holding the onion securely, carefully cut horizontally from tip to bulb but not all the way through,' Alejandra warns as I start to forget the first step, 'and finally cut the onion crossways into thin slices so you can create a small dice.

'Now you give it a shot,' she tells me.

I slaughter five onions before finally managing what might pass for a clean kill. Wiping away my tears at their passing, I suggest maybe Alejandra will use the pile of diced onion to make a French onion soup.

'Unfortunately it needs to be in rings for that.'

I've still got a lot to learn.

'Okay – time to drop in your résumé at that place on Little Bourke – I reckon you're finally ready for the Onion Test,' Alejandra says and we head for the front door, stepping over the same bag she shoved out of the way when I arrived this morning.

'My work-out gear,' Alejandra says. 'Left to remind me.'

'Didn't you say Damien is at the Fitness Centre?'

'He is.'

'Isn't he expecting to see you there?'

'We joined separate places, 'Alejandra says. 'He thought it better.'

'I didn't realise married people worked out,' I say.

'We're not married.'

I know that already but I like hearing it – over and over.

■ ■ ■

The topic of Damien hangs in the air – like the car's deodoriser – but we talk about everything else. When I start banging on about the specific number of tram routes that traverse the city, Alejandra finally folds.

'Damien asked me the other day if you and I are sleeping together.'

If she laughs next, how do I take it? If she doesn't, how do I take it?

Alejandra is driving – so theoretically she's obliged not to look at me. She sticks to the road rules like a champion.

I'm mute and I swear I can hear the clock ticking – though best as I can see there isn't one.

'I said "No, we're not sleeping together,"' Alejandra recounts, '"but we do we like hanging out and we laugh heaps."'

'Exactly,' I say.

It made no sense but I hadn't made a noise for a bit.

'He was *relieved* by that,' Alejandra says softly, as if lost in thought. So much so she gets blasted by some impatient hoon and forgets to take offence.

■ ■ ■

After parking the car we walk towards Little Bourke and pass the same Sushi Train place that I've twice left my résumé with. The same ad remains in the window and I point it out to Alejandra. She walks into the place – loads of people are sitting watching the raw fish races – and tears the notice from the inside of the front window. After ripping it into pieces she dumps it onto the conveyor belt.

Not a word said to anyone, including me.

Maybe I'll get a call from them or … maybe I won't.

■ ■ ■

'Good luck – don't forget to dice as fine as possible,' Alejandra says and I leave her outside the Sleeping Bison café.

The place is massive, busy, and its notice suggests it needs a plural of kitchen help – hence the special effort with pre-training on my part. Oh, and hanging with Alejandra at her place this morning was no great sacrifice.

I wait by the cashier's booth, résumé at the ready, wearing a collared shirt that says I'm real serious.

'Your notice says to ask for the manager?' I say, uplifting the end of the sentence to create a question, which has the effect of making me appear nice and simple.

The cashier returns with a slick-looking guy who has a disregard for regular shaving. He looks over my résumé very quickly – which is fortunate – and asks me if I'm available now for a quick competency test in the kitchen.

'No worries,' I say, a tad smarmily.

'I'm Atom,' he tells me, shaking my hand as we push through the swinging doors.

'As in the building block of the universe?'

'That's me,' Atom says.

He has quite a lot to live up to. My name simply prepares you to meet a former desk-jockey from Auto World – one who only eats chicken and keeps a single goldfish.

After pointing out an empty section on a long stainless-steel bench, Atom gives me a knife and … an artichoke.

I look at the thing – it's impossible to imagine how it's meant to be mutilated.

Atom waits impatiently.

'I only do onions,' I tell him before swinging the doors the other way.

No tears.

■ ■ ■

'I like your blouse,' Alejandra says to Joy once Travis has helped extricate his mother from the car.

Joy glances down at the white top with multicoloured circumnavigations.

'Horizontal stripes,' Joy smiles. 'Helps bulk me up a bit.'

As we walk in the direction of where we'd have preferred to park Joy tells Alejandra and Travis about her day. She's no need to tell me as I was there.

'After lunch Ethan took me to the Sakura Lounge,' Joy says. 'It's in one of those laneways in the city.'

'They do shiatsu and beauty therapies,' I explain, recalling the blurb from the website, 'and have a tatami lounge.'

'Tsunami lounge?' Travis asks.

'Tatami,' Joy says. 'You relax there after your massage – you lie down on these straw mats, in your kimonos, and drink Japanese green tea.'

There are several sushi restaurants along this section of Toorak Road and we find one not too posh and devoid of a mini-travellator doing laps before hungry punters.

'They don't throw it at you, do they?' Travis asks as we wait to be seated.

'No,' I say.

We specifically chose a place that allows Joy to try raw fish without requiring Travis to catch food that is moving.

It's not yet too crowded – like Floridians we're happy to feed early – and we eye a table in the window.

The host is not Asian and he wears what can only be described as knitwear.

'Party of four?'

Joy winks at me, 'No, it's a *gang* of four.'

'Yes thanks,' I say to the guy and we get the table we want.

After we're seated the same guy comes to collects our order.

'We haven't got our menus yet,' I say nicely enough.

'This table is booked for eight-thirty,' he mutters as he directs a Japanese girl with a ponytail to bring us menus promptly.

'Your boss is not a happy man,' Travis says to the girl and she agrees without actually saying as much.

Nobody in particular seems to be assigned to our table – our order is taken by a different girl and our entrees delivered by a cheerful young guy. They all look like university students you'd happily copy notes from. Meanwhile their boss chases them about as though he's herding cats, in between screaming, 'No takeaway!' into the phone. I can't imagine what it's like when the place is completely full. The stress is taking its toll on the workers, who are starting to deliver the wrong thing to some of our neighbouring tables.

The host snatches a plate of sashimi out of the cheerful guy's hand at one point. 'I'll take this,' he says to him, 'you're too slow.' And then he dumps it on our table.

We share the large plate of raw fish.

'I can't believe I've left it so long to try this,' Joy says. 'It's so fresh.'

'It's also very, um … tasty,' Alejandra notes.

I bet she was going to say *slimming* or *healthy* but caught herself in time.

We leave no slice of fish unturned and receive our gyoza, yakitori, sushi and miso soup from a variety of frightened attendants. The place is full now – there's even a small queue forming out front – and the host has us on the clock.

After some seaweed ice-cream the check arrives on the table and once we've loaded the small laminate tray with cash it's whisked away. Bizarrely the check seems to reappear on the table just as we are leaving – a nice arrival present for the party we've warmed seats for.

Alejandra has her ciggie in her mouth and lighter at the ready before the door has closed behind us and we linger outside the restaurant so she can ash the entire length of the thing into the gutter.

People are streaming into the place now and suddenly the waitress with the ponytail joins us on the street. She is looking very sheepish.

'Colin says you didn't pay.'

'What?' Alejandra says.

'Who's Colin?' Travis asks.

'My boss,' she says, looking down. 'He told me to tell you to pay.'

'Do you think we skipped out only to loiter on the kerb?' Alejandra asks, incredulous.

'*I* don't,' the waitress replies, reminding us, 'but Colin does.'

'It's not her fault,' I say. 'I'll check it out.'

Making my way past the annoyed-looking horde caught in the doorway, who obviously suspect I'm queue-jumping, to the cashier's station, I wait while Colin yells, 'No takeaway!' into the phone.

'You didn't pay,' he says directly.

'Yes we did,' I protest. 'Would we still be here if we hadn't?'

'Who did you pay?' he asks dubiously.

I spot the guy who'd collected our money tray and point across the restaurant at him. By this time Joy, Alejandra and Travis have also come back inside and stand behind me as if we are the Jets from *West Side Story*.

Colin calls Akira over and asks him if he remembers collecting payment from our table. Akira studies our faces and finally recollects.

'Oh yeah,' he says, pointing at Joy. 'The sick lady.'

Why not the beautiful guy? Or this merely ordinary one. Shit, even the fat girl.

Colin says to Akira, 'Go!'

And to us, 'You can go.'

'That's it?' I protest, but before Colin has a chance to respond I hear, 'RAT!'

Alejandra is pointing and moving her arm along the base of the wall, through people's legs, and shrieking 'RAT!' over and over. The place is in disarray – most everyone is trying to get their feet as far from the floor as they can. In the same confusion I'd imagine arises when someone calls 'Shark!' at a beach, the queue disappears and the only ones stuck inside are those who've eaten and genuinely not yet paid.

But we can leave as we've paid in full and they know it.

As we drive back along Toorak Road I tell Joy how disappointed I am the night had to end like that.

'Ethan – that's why I like to travel,' Joy says with a warm smile. 'It's unpredictable. I mean – a rat!'

'There was no rat,' Travis says.

'Yeah, there was,' Alejandra says, laughing.

Out the front of the grand houses we pass, cherry blossoms are basking under moonlight – well, streetlights anyway. In the distance you can just make out Mount Fuji. I blink my eyes – you'd swear I'd just been cutting onions.

28. Super Tuesday

The open call is set to commence at seven-thirty – in the morning! Presumably this race against the clock is to weed out half the aspiring railway workers from the get-go. If this were a casting for models they'd be given time to wake naturally, dress properly, and purge breakfast before being expected to parade.

I presume that the lift-loads of applicants being spilled into the bland foyer of this hotel's conference facility have all, like me, survived the initial telephone assessment. The lady who assessed my general intelligence with a few questions that insulted my general intelligence emphasised, after congratulating me on passing stage one, that I must bring with me my completed application form and dress smart-casual for today's information and testing session. Transparently this was a test to see if we could, and would, follow directions.

The modest-sized foyer quickly fills with a vast collection of sloppily dressed dorks and elegantly dressed Indians. I lean against a wall, between some guy wearing a chintz shirt with puffy shoulders – a man in a blouse – and a lady wrapped in a sapphire-coloured sari. From what I can ascertain through the immovable windows it is now well past seven-thirty but no one has arrived who looks in any way in charge of things. We are all left silently waiting in this airless and crowded foyer. As though we are stuck on a train.

A panel of elegantly dressed dorks finally arrive and ask us to follow them through to the conference room, which is vast and features a wide stage that *Hamlet* could play out on. We are encouraged to take seats towards the front and ironically more than one attendee decides now is a good time to put their feet on the seats and munch on the pop-tarts and breakfast bars they've liberated from their backpacks. I'm sensing some of my comrades are here simply to enable them to tick a box at Centrelink.

'Welcome everybody and thanks for coming here to our information and testing session,' an impressive-looking woman tells her microphone. Her colleagues sit facing us along a trestle table covered with a white sheet, like some sort of wedding party. The bride goes on to explain what gaining an entry-level role at the railways entails and how this morning will proceed – general questions, then three levels of testing – with people weeded out each round, and then the prize: an appointment for a health test for anyone who makes it over all hurdles.

'Can I check that everyone has brought along their completed application forms?' the bride asks.

A hand goes up.

One row in front of me a girl dressed for a blizzard asks, 'The form states you must provide three references but I don't have that many.'

The groom puts his face into his microphone.

'How many jobs have you had previously?'

'Four. But I left three of those without actually telling them.'

The rest of the wedding party attempts to suppress their smiles.

'Just do the best you can,' he says groomily.

Blizzard's friend is taking a photo of the chandelier with her mobile.

Alongside me a guy whose swollen gut definitely makes him

look qualified to work on the railways asks, 'Is it possible, with these tests you give us, to be *too* smart?'

'That won't be a problem,' the bridesmaid holding the test papers says flatly.

■ ■ ■

I was voted off *Railways Survivor* after the third stage of testing. Only about half-a-dozen remained at the end. They all look well chuffed – their train had finally arrived.

Walking to Centrelink I'm not surprised that I recognise several of the people I've just battled with. My fellow railway dropouts all seem to know their way around the job boards and queues; however, as this is my first time I wait at the information desk for a break in the personal phone calls.

'I haven't applied for the dole before,' I explain to the first person who accidentally catches my eye.

'Job Search Allowance,' the lady corrects me before handing over a form and telling me to wait in the longest queue they have going.

The place reminds me of VicRoads or Medicare; as with all government departments there are a lot of empty desks, unanswered phones, and an obligatory alcoholic guy wearing a Hawaiian shirt. Alco-pop tells me, after reviewing my financials, that due to the rent I receive from my father's old house in Keilor East I'm getting zip.

■ ■ ■

The only thing more hideous than looking for work is passing time at Federation Square: obnoxious tourists and obnoxious locals. I have ten minutes before my interview, arranged via Seek, at SBS Television. Not fully aware what the role of data controller in the news library might involve, it's impossible to prepare any further. The ad did say that flexible work hours were on offer and a familiarity with world events would be highly advantageous. To that end, during my last session at the internet café – doctoring my résumé repeatedly and sending it off to an even wider spectrum of jobs than previously – I caught up on all things Barack and Iraq.

Upon being directed through the SBS corridors, adorned with glamorous publicity shots of the network's celebrities, I now sit facing one set of sleepy eyes and another pair slightly more awake and separated by a nose burdened with an unsightly mole. The guy with the drooping eyes would be my manager and the mole is from HR.

'This particular position is to man the news desk during the hours that our local operations are officially shut down.'

I must still look a little unsure so Sleepy continues.

'Most of the big international news events unfold whilst we in Australia are asleep, so we need to have someone here keeping an eye on the feeds from Reuters, ITN, AAP and the BBC. If anything *really big* breaks then you call our news director, irrespective of the time.'

'Is someone doing this job at the moment?' I ask.

'Me,' Sleepy says.

'Do you think you could handle the hours?' the HR lady asks me.

'Yes. I think so.'

In fact, merely watching television feeds from around the world, on the off chance some idiot shoots Obama or some hero finds Osama, sounds straightforward enough.

'Obviously, the time can also be spent listing shots from the news tapes we receive daily into our database.'

And there's the catch.

Sleepy continues, 'Our journalists need to find useful shots quickly – for example, Hillary shaking hands with Karzai, or Israeli troops in the West Bank – when they're compiling background pieces.'

Sleepy and HR both have a printed copy of my résumé in front of them. Unfortunately I've no idea what version I sent with my initial application. It could include all of my last few jobs – all listed as '2009' – or just those I thought related to this job in some tenuous way, or none at all after my only long-term position at Auto World. Maybe they got the résumé which claims I've been travelling since my father died. Which isn't entirely a lie.

We talk about Auto World for a bit. And then, 'And what did you do next, Ethan?' Sleepy says, looking blearily at my résumé.

I pause – trying to read through the back of the single sheet.

'What does it say?' I ask.

■ ■ ■

'Let's start you straight away – see how you go.'

Unfortunately this is not SBS; they terminated my interview quite abruptly, so now I've gone to the dogs.

The midweek meet at the track is not yet officially open – even most of the greyhounds are still at home preparing for their big night out – but the snack bar is already simmering with anticipation.

Marvin, tonight's boss, has reached an age and size where his chest has turned into breasts. I can't imagine the menu in this place is doing him any favours. He instructs me to load the Coke fridge with Pepsi and the Heinz ketchup bottles with generic. Troy, just a few days my senior from what I can ascertain, is unpacking pre-skewered kebab sticks to the sound of a symphony of frying snacks: fish cocktails, onion rings, crab sticks, and chicken nuggets.

'What should I do now?' I ask Marvin, who is overseeing the rotisserie chickens.

'Make sure we have everything on the condiments table and then you can start filling the server with the stuff that's done frying.'

It seems food preparation in this place is mostly about unpacking and basic assemblage. Like furniture from Ikea. No onions need dicing and I bet they've never even seen an artichoke. This could be it!

The best part about the job – aside from the fact we're allowed to eat anything we like as we work – is that there is in fact plenty to do. Time passes quickly and before I know it my shirt is permanently ruined with fat splatters and the track announcer is calling the first race.

Half an hour before his heart attack a bear of a man asks me for three crab sticks, half-a-dozen nuggets, two burgers, large chips with gravy, and a diet Pepsi. From what I can tell he's going to eat this all himself at the laminate credenza a few metres away. He douses the lot with chicken salt. Except the Pepsi of course – he can't get the salt in the can. Already the condiments table – butter, salts, sauces – has seen more spillage that the Exxon Valdez and is becoming a slush of additives.

'That's not a fucking large chips!'

Troy is under fire.

A woman who has just fallen out of bed shoves her carton of chips back at Troy, who relents and balances another full scoop atop the portion. The woman snatches it back and hits the free condiments. She's a big fan of vinegar.

My line seems to be longer than Troy's and I worry he is faster than me. Marvin, like any good boss, has disappeared.

'Two quarter-chicken and chips.'

Please is heard less here than in the army.

'So, half a chicken with chips?' I ask, hoping to cut to the chase and not be the slowest purveyor of death accelerators this side of the counter.

'NO! Two *quarter*-chickens,' the guy screams. 'I want both the wings.'

Who chooses wings?

In fact, they prove very popular here amongst a crowd which, if *they* were birds, would all be flightless. One of my customers actually orders 'the wings of three chickens' and several repeat the joke about taking any part of the chicken so long as it's not the nuggets.

Eventually I realise what is going on here: the crowd is wise to the fact Troy is that most despised of all fast-food attendants – the light ladler. From what I've observed he's yet to eat anything himself, in spite of it being free, and he's a little stingy with the feeders as well.

I cut back on my portion sizes so the disparity is not so obvious and over the next two hours the lengths of our lines balance out a bit.

Marvin returns and I get the first break. I decide to scoot over to the stands to watch an actual race, otherwise I'd feel a bit like those people who spend a day at the beach without ever getting wet. Taking a seat in the back row I slouch back and wait for the starting boxes to entice the dogs inside.

'Hey.' A blond guy with tattoos, who is on his way up the steps, stops and looks down at me.

'Hey,' I say.

'Don't you remember me?' he says.

'Um …'

'It's Guy. From The Book Place,' he says. 'With the greyhound.'

'Oh, sure,' I say, suddenly remembering him from the ciggie breaks with Alejandra. 'The guy with the greyhound.'

'Yeah – *Guy* with the greyhound.'

'So what are you doing here?'

'Guy … with the *greyhound*,' he says with a grin.

'Oh yeah.'

'What about you?' he asks me, taking a seat.

'I just started work at the snack bar inside,' I reply, a little embarrassed.

'How do you like it?'

'The *clientele* are a little hard to satisfy.'

'I bet,' Guy says laughing.

'So, your dog is running tonight?'

'Yeah – not this race but the next.' I notice Guy has a fine coating of sweat across his forehead. 'I'm a bit nervous actually.'

'What's his name?'

'Bunny Muncher,' Guy replies.

And to think I'm occasionally bothered by the name Grout.

'Why don't you come down and watch me load him in?' Guy says. 'You can't see much from up here.'

'Okay,' I say.

It's pretty obvious Guy is here alone and could do with someone familiar to watch the race with. I can relate to that.

■ ■ ■

Guy's dog comes third – no bunny munching tonight. Marvin gives me a right bollocking for coming back late from my break. Troy continues to outscrimp me, and my line never shortens. Someone throws the top of their burger bun back at me – it had mould on it. The condiment table requires wiping down over thirty times. Grease has caused my shirt to become see-through. My tips add up to zero. This sucks … and farewell.

29. The Insider Buzz

Again I find myself here.

The flimsy partition that has been erected to put some dignity between those of us squirming in anticipation and the unseen person squirming through interrogation is not up to the task.

'*And* this office is very convenient for me,' the woman lists her final selling point.

'I'm pleased,' the man's expressionless voice says.

She did a lot better on the 'what book are you reading' question. So much so that I'm nearly distracted from eavesdropping by the brain-racking I need to do to prepare myself for that one.

Next to me – my other competition – is sweating bullets. I decide to open a window – I'm sure he could do with some fresh air, and I'd also like to ascertain if they do in fact open – which they do. This building can breathe. I want the job.

The man behind the felt-covered wall is explaining what is involved in being his assistant, and the woman interjects to note the main aspect of the job that interests her. 'Oh, I love reading – all my girlfriends are in book clubs.'

'You won't really be reading for enjoyment on work time – you realise that?'

She didn't.

Encouraged to extrapolate on the convenience aspect of her previous reply the woman explains, 'I can easily drop off and collect my kids on my way here and the way home,' she says excitedly. 'On the days I work.'

'The ad did say this was a full-time position – office hours,' the man says. 'So school runs will be a bit difficult.'

'You don't understand,' the woman says, and I lean forward so as not to miss this, 'I have incredible attention to detail and am *personally* offended if I ever fail to deliver.'

She can't believe the guy doesn't recognise her self-evident sparkle.

'We need someone to be personally offended by their mistakes five full days a week,' he says.

After the woman leaves my waiting room companion peeks around the partition and is hastened inside by the voice. The handshake sounds like it goes awkwardly and then I spot a bee make its way through the open window and over the barricade. The commotion one little bee can cause is amazing. Seems the sweaty guy held out too long before attempting to swipe it away and the interview is spent with the prospective boss marveling intermittently on the rapid swelling taking place on his forehead.

'You're up,' the man with the bump tells me before quitting this place for a medical centre.

The voice, as it transpires, belongs to a friendly looking man stuffed inside a sandstone-coloured cardigan. He stands to offer an outstretched hand and before I remind myself to look him in the eyes I note his lazy shoes. The velcro straps look a little frayed but they're clinging on.

'Hi Ethan,' he says, after glancing at his agenda, 'I'm Leon.'

'Hey.'

I use my empty, just-for-effect document holder to swipe a dead bee off the table.

'Seems you have a friend who's been looking out for you,' Leon says, but I feign ignorance at the whole kerfuffle that preceded me. But he is right, in a way.

'Let's get started,' Leon says, 'As you'll recall from our advert ...'

I never saw the advert.

'... I'm one of the publishers at Tate Lane and we require someone to assist me with various duties.'

'Yes,' I say.

'Now, as it happens, I can't actually recall your résumé ...'

I never sent it.

'... there were so many and I had one of my colleague's assistants collate the interview agenda. We lend out our assistants to each other when we're stuck.'

'That makes it sound like we see off a lot of assistants, doesn't it?' Leon adds.

'It does a bit.'

'So,' Leon continues, 'the upshot is that I'm unfamiliar with your experience. Do you have a copy of your resume there?'

Leon nods at my document-free document-holder and I freeze.

'Why don't you just tell me about your last position?'

The trip from The Book Place to here is short and sweet and I make no stops in between.

'I'm sure my colleague's assistant also used to work at The Book Place before it got swallowed,' Leon says to my blank face. 'Alejandra Garcia?'

I stick with blank.

'Do you know her from your time there?'

'I think so,' I rub my chin for a bit, 'vaguely.'

'That's quite a coincidence,' Leon says.

Not *too* much of a coincidence I hope.

'Now Ethan,' Leon, is no conspiracy theorist fortunately, and moves on, 'do you like to read?'

'Books?'

'Yes. Books.'

'Uh-huh.'

'What was the last book you read?'

Alejandra suggested, in our hastily organised training session earlier, naming a book Tate Lane has the rights to and, though she had a suspicion Leon may not be a literary snob like her own boss, it's better to play it safe.

'*To Kill a Mockingbird.*'

'That sounds like a book you read at school.'

'No, I watched the movie for school … just reading the book now.'

'What are some of your favourite novels?'

Fuck – I'd only prepared for one, not a list.

'*Fight Club.*'

Silence.

'*Trainspotting.*'

Silence.

'*Revolutionary Road.*'

'Any books that are *not* movies, Ethan?' Leon asks with the hint of a smile.

I'm getting the impression that though these may sound like wrong answers they're earning the body language and facial expressions of just the opposite. If I get this gig it wouldn't be the first time I've gotten a job because I've come across as the antithesis of a go-getter. The lack of strong competition offered by my dupe co-applicants will likely have played its part as well. Basically I'll be that guy in the Winter Olympics ice-skating race who wins because everyone in front of him falls over.

'Seems all good books are being filmed nowadays,' I say unconvincingly, but he seems not to mind.

Leon tells me, 'I'll be making my decision very shortly.'

This is my cue to leave so I stand up, collect my air-filled folder, and Leon, looking at the stingless bee that I'm likely to stand on, warns, 'Don't forget your helpful friend.'

No chance. I'm going to call her the minute I get out of here.

'So, is Alejandra excited about you working with her again?'

'She sounded like it – I'd only just finished thanking her for lining up the interview when my new boss called to offer me the job,' I tell Joy as she steadies herself with the oxygen pole.

I pour the teriyaki over the chicken and there you have it – teriyaki chicken.

'Thank goodness for jars,' I say.

Joy laughs – she won't eat much of this but whatever's left won't last long once Travis gets home. It's been a few weeks since we visited the sights of Tokyo and now we're making do with creating a little bit of the Orient at home.

'So is your palliative nurse nice?'

'She's lovely,' Joy says. 'Not as lovely as you know who though.'

I know who.

'Not sure I'm such a fan of Damien,' Joy tells me.

'You've never met him,' I say.

'No matter. Alejandra has filled me in.'

'She has?'

'Take it from me,' Joy says pointedly, 'she's not married to that one!'

'I know that.'

But it's nice to hear all the same.

Travis joins us just as I'm done clearing away the plates – one empty and one that I merely reroute to him. He hoes in immediately and raves to Joy about the meal, though he knows full well it was me who dumped the sauce on the bird.

'It was all Ethan's doing,' Joy tells him.

'Still tastes good,' Travis says, smiling at me.

As Travis devours his dinner both Joy and I watch him in silence for a bit, then I break first.

'Are you doing anything tonight?' I ask Travis.

'Sure am,' he replies.

'What?' I ask.

'Hanging with you guys.'

30. Pulp

'Blue or black?'

'What?' I say.

'Pens,' the girl empowered to dispense stationery says impatiently. 'Blue or black?'

'Blue.'

'You can have a whole box if you wish.'

'Nah,' I say. 'That won't be necessary.'

I also score a wad of notepads and an industrial-sized stapler that surgeons might use for gastric-bypass surgery.

'My name's Ethan by the way.'

Alejandra didn't introduce me for fear people will make the connection. Fact is, I doubt I'm ever going to make the connection.

'Three hundred and thirty,' the receptionist says.

I look at her. She looks human. But now that I think about it, her plundering of the stationery cupboard was a tad robotic.

'I'm just temporary,' Robot 330 says. 'You'll know me as 330 – that's how the phone announces me when I divert calls through.'

I walk past last week's interrogation room and take the lift up to where all the offices are. Presumably they'll be familiar. With offices, like Maccas, you usually know what you're gonna get. The lift still smells of a fragrance Alejandra referred to as belonging to Celeste Gray. Her boss. Apparently she arrives before everyone else and establishes her dominance by scenting the lift for everyone who comes after.

'It's Poison,' Alejandra told me.

'So you smell her before you see her,' I said to Alejandra as she kicked me out at the publisher's reception desk after our clandestine meet-for-coffee around the corner. 'Like a dead rodent stuck behind your oven.'

Actually Alejandra calls her *The* Celeste Gray, which makes her sound like a ship.

Mostly Alejandra talked work over coffee this morning, thinking I cared for all the background noise when I had her in my foreground again. She warned me that most of her colleagues are super-keen and Tate Lane is their entire reason for drawing breath.

'I'm not at work,' she told me in a covert whisper, 'I'm in a cult.'

As I leave the lift with my stationery supplies and walk down the long corridor, which is lined both sides with small dens overwhelmed by floor-to-ceiling shelving that is in turn overwhelmed by books and books-in-progress, Celeste's scent seems to get stronger rather than diminish. I glance briefly into each space as I pass – 330 told me that Leon's office is the tenth on the right but I forgot to initiate a count.

'Hello?'

A stack of paper is speaking in a woman's voice.

'Hi,' I say. 'I'm looking for Leon.'

'You don't hear that often,' the stack says, before a face rises above it. 'Celeste Gray,' says a lady with expensive-looking dark hair as she stands up, smiling confidently at me. She has even more snap than Sarah Palin.

Spread over the desk is what appears to be a hard-copy manuscript she's working on. There's also an artillery of crisply sharp pencils splayed out before her.

'Ethan Grout,' I say, accepting her offered hand and giving it the fair sort of shake she looks like she'd respect.

'The new assistant?' Celeste asks.

'Uh-huh,' I say.

'Tell me, Ethan,' Celeste says, getting straight into it as Alejandra had predicted, 'what are you reading?'

The future?

'*Then We Came To The End*. Joshua Ferris,' I reply.

'One of ours,' Celeste says approvingly.

Alejandra gave me that one. Not the book. The tip.

'Alejandra!' Celeste suddenly calls.

Alejandra walks in and we avoid looking at each other.

'This is Ethan Grout,' Celeste introduces us, 'Leon's latest offsider.'

I let Alejandra take the lead – I'm not sure how's she going to play this.

'Alejandra,' Alejandra says blankly. 'I'm Celeste's assistant.'

'Hi,' I say.

'Do you have the advances of T.C.'s book yet?' Celeste asks Alejandra reproachfully.

I recall that T.C. Bryce is the author who likes to reduce Alejandra to a mere Sandra.

'I'm told they'll be here on time,' Alejandra replies from the doorway.

'The problem being, Alejandra, that "on time" seems to mean little to you,' Celeste growls, and then suddenly returns to the manuscript her pencil was lashing out at before I arrived. She slashes away at the manuscript a bit more, whilst we both stand there unsure if we are released. It's like she's pruning a grapevine infected with rot. I'm guessing this power display is for my benefit.

'Alejandra, how are we to ensure you don't miss eight-thirty meetings?'

'By not holding eight-thirty meetings,' Alejandra replies.

I suppress a grin.

'Those team meetings have been around since well before you arrived and will continue long after you've gone,' Celeste predicts. 'While we have the pleasure of your company here they *are* mandatory!'

Celeste is now as chilled as someone going cold turkey off coffee, cigarettes and chocolate simultaneously.

'T.C.'s launch is at five,' Celeste reminds Alejandra, casting a critical eye from head to toe, silent but deadly – like poison. 'As anyone who matters from the media, and from here, will be in attendance, *so* must the book.'

Alejandra told me this morning she is not on that invitation list even though she was the one who pushed the novel though its final stages of production.

'Anyway,' I say finally, 'I'd better find Leon.'

'Take her with you.' Celeste's waves her pencil in the direction of the door.

'Welcome to Tate Lane,' Alejandra says with a smile once we are in the corridor. 'I bet you're not so sure now that you want to thank me.'

For me the positive still outweighs the negative.

Alejandra points out Leon's door before disappearing into her own.

Leon welcomes me and, to explain my tardiness, I tell him, 'I met Celeste Gray.'

'Her cat's on Prozac,' Leon says, as if this clarifies everything.

■ ■ ■

'So, what are you reading at the moment?'

And again, '*Then We Came To The End*. Joshua Ferris.'

At this rate I'm going to have to find a copy of the book – or at the very least check out what Amazon has got to say about it. Actually reading the thing might be overkill at this early juncture.

Cameron, the sales manager who's just introduced himself, looks satisfied at my selection of reading material and takes his place at the boardroom table. He wears one of those charity bracelets – today he's green.

Celeste leans across the table toward Cameron and says, none too softly, 'Can you believe Leon has chosen an assistant who *reads?*'

The table fills quickly for what Leon told me is the 'Big Meeting', which follows each team's 'Small Meeting' and brings the various departments together once a week.

'Everyone needs to be kept in the loop,' Leon explained as we trooped downstairs.

Assistants don't sit at the table apparently – chairs ring the walls from where we can keep an eye on our manager's backs. Alejandra is the last to arrive and leaves an empty chair between us. Though she gives me the smile of someone who thinks she's invisible.

A curmudgeon, who Celeste earlier lunged to sit next to, opens proceedings. Maybe this is Tate Lane himself. Or maybe it's a place. I've no idea.

'Let's get into it,' he harrumphs before deferring to another man, 'Star?'

Alejandra is at my ear. 'Star Cherry, publishing director. Big mystery what Star is short for.'

Nice summation.

'All the sales team should have the latest catalogue and stocklist.' Star Cherry looks to Cameron to validate this, which he does. 'A few problems though – let me guide us through, shall I?'

Alejandra slips me a scrap of paper that says *Starlet?*

'Veronica – did you oversee the categorisations?'

Veronica, blonde ringlets and nervous demeanour, is on the other side of Alejandra.

'Um. Yes.'

'*I Know Why The Caged Bird Sings.*' Star Cherry creates effect by leaving this hanging in the air for a few beats.

Starfish? Alejandra's fresh note says.

'Which category do you think this particular modern American classic found its way into?' Star Cherry asks the A-team at the table while us reserves, except the ringletted one, are well pleased it's not us in the headlights.

'Pets and Nature!' Star Cherry says.

There is some laughter at the table, and some horror, depending if you are anarchist or true believer. Celeste isn't smiling, while Cameron is shakily trying to recall the last funeral he attended or the plight of the refugees in Darfur.

My boss, Leon, has no expression at all so I can't gauge where he fits into all of this.

Starfucker?

I suppress a smile.

Star Cherry continues, 'It found its way to sit alongside titles on dog training, bird spotting and chicken-raising!'

Humiliation complete.

Tate Lane himself has been flicking through his copy of the stocklist with a look of bewilderment that's causing further drag on his deeply lined face.

'Star, I don't know what half of these categories are.'

'We tried to modernise the groupings to better suit our list and the emerging trends.' Star Cherry speaks on behalf of all the publishers.

Starburst?

'Chick Lit, Lad Lit, Matron Lit and Grit Lit,' Tate Lane says. 'I get these but what is Trick Lit?'

'Fictionalised diaries of prostitutes,' Star Cherry replies.

'This is a category?'

'Yes.'

'And we publish in this category?'

'Yes.'

'Hick Lit?'

'Stories with rural settings.'

'Layoff Lit?'

'Hard times.'

'Woto?'

'Women overcoming the odds.'

'What did we used to call those?' Tate Lane asks, exasperated.

'Biographies,' Star Cherry replies.

'And there was a problem with that?'

Tate Lane mutters to himself for a bit and then Star Cherry commences asking each of the publishers in turn what is on their agenda for the week.

'*I Lick My Cheese.*'

Weirdly no one looks at all surprised at this frank statement from the woman whose throat wears a belt of black pearls.

'What's that one again?' Star Cherry asks her.

'The collection of flat-sharing anecdotes,' she replies, speaking as quickly as the disclaimer they run at the end of pharmaceutical ads. 'I'll finish the final edit this week and Veronica will get it to production.'

'*Mandela: A Life.*'

The woman sat next to the cheese-licker explains further, 'This homage to the life of a great man has come together beautifully. We're just running the photographs through the rights department now.'

'He's dead?' Tate Lane asks.

'No,' the woman explains. 'Not quite. It's best to be ready though – we've done a generic layout for the final chapter.'

The race is on – Castro versus Mandela.

'Who will you get to do the foreword?' Star Cherry asks her.

'We'll go through the standard list: Dalai Lama, Deepak Chopra, Edward De Bono, Desmond Tutu.'

'Leon?'

Now I get to hear what I'll be working on.

'Jared Lindstrom has just delivered his manuscript,' Leon says.

'Can I get a copy?' Star Cherry asks excitedly.

'To read?' Leon asks.

'Yes.' Star Cherry replies. 'To *read*.'

Celeste laughs for Tate Lane's benefit.

'What's it like?' Cameron asks Leon. 'His first was huge for us in sales – if this is anything like it we'll be laughing.'

'You won't be laughing,' Leon warns. 'The editor I've assigned to it reckons this is his *Crocodile Dundee 2*.'

'You're not doing the edit yourself?' Star Cherry asks Leon.

Celeste further straightens her already broomstick-like spine.

'I'm focusing on my own stuff,' Leon says.

'Which is?' Star Cherry asks.

'Paranormal Romance.'

'What?' Tate Lane shouts.

'Vampires,' Leon explains.

'Why not,' Tate Lane mumbles to himself.

The lady who publishes lifestyle books goes next and its all Gordon this and Nigella that.

'Finally, Celeste?' Star Cherry says.

'It's all about T.C. Bryce this week,' Celeste explains. 'Tonight we have the launch at Movida. T.C. and some other guests will come here first for pre-dinner drinks. This will enable publicity to have T.C. sign a few promotional copies.'

'Great work, Celeste,' Star Cherry determines. 'I haven't seen a copy yet though.'

'Alejandra's ensuring the advances arrive in time,' Celeste assures him, '*as we speak*.'

In fact, Alejandra is currently scribbling her latest version of Star Cherry's first name *as we speak*. *Startle*.

'So who is coming in for the drinks beforehand?'

Celeste starts listing the select authors and T.C. hangers-on when the lifestyle publisher interjects, proudly boasting, 'I can deliver Jamie!'

'Jamie Oliver is in town?' Star Cherry looks impressed.

'Durie.'

'Oh.'

Leon, upon Celeste's request, allows me to spend the afternoon helping Alejandra set up the rooftop terrace for the pre-dinner drinks.

'So, how many people are they expecting?'

'About thirty for drinks and a hundred or so for dinner,' Alejandra replies. 'They've booked the entire restaurant.'

We ensure the fridges are stocked and sweep the terrace free of leaves before scattering tables and chairs in a haphazard formation. Then we sit down in the afternoon sun for Alejandra's ciggie break.

'So will I get to meet the famous T.C. Bryce this afternoon?' I ask as Alejandra puts her feet on the same side table that mine hold down.

'I think we are meant to keep glasses filled whilst not getting in the way,' Alejandra tells me. 'So, what do you think of Leon?'

'I still haven't really had much time with him yet,' I reply, 'though I have to say he seems the least driven of the publishers.'

'Leon is actually the son-in-law – he married into this place.'

'Ah,' I say.

'Whereas The Celeste Gray is married *to* this place.'

'She does appear very excited about tonight,' I note.

'Celeste will remain until the very last light is extinguished,' Alejandra says. 'Like a moth.'

We return briefly to our computers to log off before we can start popping corks off the roof. I'm surprised to see my first email. I'm even more surprised to see what it's telling me.

PS. I love you.

… And it's from Cameron, the sales guy from the Big Meeting.

Immediately I seek out Alejandra but she is helping a girl, as slim as everyone else in publicity, schlep boxes of T.C. Bryce's book to the terrace. I help out but cannot get Alejandra to myself before thirsty people start arriving. Veronica and I are directed by Celeste to man the makeshift bar while Alejandra and the thinnest of all the publicists prepare the signing table just metres away.

Finally Alejandra joins the bar crew but Veronica gets in the way of me mentioning the email from Cameron. A grungy-looking dude comes up for a beer and Alejandra introduces me to Jared Lindstrom – the author whose second book Leon passed onto an editor for overhauling.

'How long did it take you to write your first book?' I ask, focusing on his proven bestseller – it was Oprah'd apparently.

'Seventy-two hours thirty-five minutes,' Jared Lindstrom replies.

'That's quick.'

'Over five years.'

'Sounds a tough life – writing books,' I say.

'A bigger challenge is finding people for the dedication,' he replies before walking his beer outside.

I still haven't had an opportunity to tell Alejandra about *the* email, which I'm going to assume came to me by mistake – Cameron's not quite good-looking enough to be gay.

After sending a seriously ancient lady off with a considerably younger vintage of wine, I look up to see Cameron standing there. My face selects the red.

'Did you get my email, Ethan?' Cameron asks nonchalantly.

'Um,' I say eloquently. 'I've sort of been helping out here.'

'We need a local reprint ordered for one of Leon's books,' Cameron says.

Okay. We're on *different* emails here.

'*PS. I Love You.*'

'That's a book?'

Before I have a chance to glass myself in the face I am distracted by a fuss whipping up the stairs. Celeste appears with a hard-looking man who must be her beloved T.C. Bryce. He is marginally younger than I'd imagined, classically attired, and moaning about his flight.

'… she, wider than the aisle, is standing there telling me would *I care* to turn my mobile off …'

Celeste nods emphatically.

'… so I tell her we could all bring an extra carry-on bag if she'd only *care* to drop some kilos.'

This, apparently, is the wittiest thing Celeste has ever heard.

'At least she wasn't squeezed in next to you,' Celeste tells first-class T.C.

'Bag and body weight should be combined. If you exceed appropriate body mass then no bags,' T.C. announces.

Veronica has disappeared; however, now that I finally have Alejandra to myself the Cameron story has lost its bite entirely.

'So that's him?' I say, nodding toward T.C. Bryce, who is settling behind a pile of his new books.

'That's the one,' Alejandra says with a smile.

'What's this novel like?'

'Pages 450 to 497.'

'What do you mean?'

'That's all I'm saying,' Alejandra says.

The emaciated publicist is walking T.C. through the dedications she wants him to place on each copy's title page and decides to engage him in conversation.

'So are your family and friends excited about reading your new work?'

'They expect to find themselves in every book I do,' T.C. Bryce tells her. 'I tell them – "FICTION!"'

The publicist jumps out of her near-empty skin, then looks relieved when Leon takes this opportunity to meet T.C. Bryce, given Celeste is busy getting her prize stallion a drink.

'What do you do publish?' T.C. asks Leon.

'I'm working on filling the voids we have in some of the fresher fiction categories that are stealing the market nowadays,' Leon tells him.

Alejandra nudges me as if to say, *This should be good.*

'What *new* categories?' T.C. Bryce growls.

'Paranormal romance, new-wave fantasy, comedic-horror, retro-gothic … you know the thing,' Leon says.

From what I can see T.C. Bryce does not know the thing.

'Do you think my *genre* is *passé*?'

'C'est la vie,' Alejandra says to me.

'Que Sera, Sera,' I reply.

Leon wanders back outside, defeated, and T.C. Bryce looks up towards us.

'SANDRA!'

Alejandra heads over to the table.

'Sandra, where are my personal copies?' T.C. Bryce shouts, though she's right in front of him.

'As agreed they are being shipped to your home.'

'Who agreed that?'

'We agreed that.'

He views her suspiciously and Celeste, standing behind him while proffering a flute, waves for Alejandra to disappear.

The publicist tries to remove all the books now that the signing is done but T.C. Bryce wrestles one back and the publicist quickly gives it up as lost. I guess it must be pretty exciting reading your own work in finished form for the first time – no matter how often you've been published. For some reason Alejandra seems excited too.

T.C. Bryce flicks through the pages and suddenly halts.

'WHAT THE FUCK IS THIS?'

31. All in a Name

The lift smells of Celeste. She's already in play.

'Have you finalised that advert yet, Ethan?'

'Design said they'll send it through this morning. Once we've checked it I'll forward it to the paper,' I tell Celeste as I pass her office, itching to log on to my computer to see if there's been an overnight email from Alejandra.

Nothing in over a week.

Not a word since T.C. Bryce discovered the spunkiest character in his latest novel had changed her name, last minute, to Alejandra. One swift 'replace all' and now Alejandra's being replaced as well. She told me not to stuff my job on account of her and I didn't tell her that my only reason for working here *was* on account of her. If I do hear from Alejandra again I won't mention it's me Celeste now orders about, hijacking half my Leon time. Moreover, irony has me overseeing the search for Alejandra's permanent replacement.

'How are you going with exotic locations?' my *other* boss, suddenly at my door, asks me in a lowered voice.

'I'm still separating the full list into islands, mountains, resorts, cities, rural, blah, blah, blah,' I tell Leon.

'Forge on,' he reminds me and is gone.

Originally I assumed I'd be sending manuscripts through to production and constructing letters to disappoint those who've toiled to produce the packages that pile in relentlessly. That was until the end of last week when Leon covertly introduced me to 'The Happy Author'. Apparently he has spent the last few years designing a sophisticated computer programme that will eventually automate the book-writing process. Then Leon need not deal with authors, let alone pay them anything.

He needs me to load into his programme as many variations of exotic locations for romance as I can think of – frankly the possibilities are endless.

The only other thing he's had me do is to check any manuscripts that get dumped onto his desk — chiefly by dropping random phrases from them into Google to see if they've met already. Leon's great fear, other than his father-in-law's wrath, is that he might reject a great piece of literature. Star Cherry has warned all the publishers that he's heard rumours that Sage & Scribner, Tate Lane's Sydney-based arch rival, is planning to bombard Tate Lane's mailroom with manuscripts that are in fact classic works submitted under pseudonyms. This in the hope we will send off a formulaic rejection letter that will belittle us when reproduced in the mainstream press that Sage & Scribner happens to own a great slab of. What serious author would want to be published by the house that had failed to recognise *and* just rejected *Cloudstreet* or *The Great Gatsby*?

■ ■ ■

'Ethan, you know what T.C. Bryce looks like, don't you?' Celeste asks me, looking out the vast windows of Star Cherry's impressive corner office.

He looks angry so far as I recall.

'Yes,' I say, handing over the printout of the advert seeking Alejandra's replacement for her approval. Celeste hasn't been hard to locate, what with her Poison, but I am surprised she's assumed Star Cherry's office whilst he's out to lunch.

The advert is quite large for such a lowly role and, as I understand it, is being prominently featured in the *Age*'s arts section. Apparently, Celeste wants to make a statement.

And another it seems. 'This will be *my* office one day,' she says when she turns around and notices my bemused expression.

I look at her. She doesn't anticipate a reply from me so I let her dream well enough alone.

'T.C.'s in Melbourne for the weekend,' she continues. 'Events and media. We've put him up at the Clarion.'

'Uh-huh,' I say.

'Rumour has it …'

Man, there are a lot of rumours in this industry.

'… that the publishing director from Sage & Scribner is also in Melbourne this weekend.'

Celeste looks at me but I've got nothing but vapid to offer.

She points to a particular framed photo on Star Cherry's wall.

'That's her, Deborah Fimmel, getting chummy with Star at Book Expo America.'

'Okay.'

'Take a good look,' she instructs me.

'Why am I looking at this?' I ask.

'Deborah Fimmel is also staying at the Clarion,' Celeste says. 'I've checked.'

'And?'

'They're trying to poach T.C.' Celeste spits it out. 'I'm sure of it.'

'What can you do about it?' I say.

'I can't be caught on the hop, that's what,' Celeste tells me, turning back to the view. 'I need you to keep an eye on things for me.'

This is not in the job description for publisher's assistant, I'm sure of it. I mean, I've got the advert in my hand.

'You want me to stake out the hotel?' I say it out loud so Celeste will recognise the lunacy.

'Yes,' she says defiantly, 'I do.'

I'm heading into a marriage with Mata Hari.

'There's a nice bar in the foyer.' She starts painting this as a fun, relaxing weekend. 'You can order food – whatever you like.'

Do they do a nice 52?

'The whole weekend?' I ask, incredulous. 'What about showers?'

Maybe she'll offer me a vial of Poison to cover any odours.

'I'm *sure* you've lasted a weekend without a shower before.'

Cheers.

'Anyway, if you see them arrive or depart together, or meet up for a drink, after you've ascertained as much as you can, then you are free to go.'

The Celeste Gray is sinking.

Star Cherry can be heard making his way down the corridor and I follow Celeste nimbly out of his office. Thankfully he engages her in some discussion and I head for my computer. Suddenly it makes sense to amend this advert slightly before clicking it through to the paper.

■ ■ ■

I lie on my bed. The nights are warm now and my open window lets in all the sirens, screeching and shouting this big city can create. Travis is no longer on the billboard and Alejandra isn't within view either. I tell Mister Fantastic it's too risky to get him some new friends. They never seem to last.

32. Forza Gang

Scooting past the obligatory reality crew filming in the corridor I hit the nurse's station like someone who's just hoovered through the drug cabinet's stash.

'I'm here to see a patient.' I'm trying not to shout. 'Joy Lever.'

The nurse wearing Sebastian's name badge asks, 'Are you family?'

'Yes. Yes, I am,' I reply, a little too defensively.

He points me in the direction of Joy's room and I take a deep breath before entering.

Travis is sitting beside Joy's bed, holding her hand. They both look at me and smile.

'How are you doing?' I ask Joy, attempting to sound light.

'I feel fine,' Joy tells me slowly, lifting her head slightly before dropping it again.

Unfortunately this is a lie.

Only one tube connects Joy to machinery and fewer coloured lights than I'd imagined are empowered to blink her message to the world. Next to the bed is the digital photo frame Travis recently set up for Joy at home, scanning in loads of her old photos and weaving in recent ones.

I sit on the edge of the bed watching as Joy lunches with friends; Travis tries to walk – first as a one year old, next as a model; Diego's head peeks out of a bag; Joy cuts a white cake with my father; I hold a traffic sign named *SLOW*; and the four of us attempt to catch food in little red bowls – three of us successfully.

Sebastian and a doctor enter the room. The doctor looks at me watching Joy's life flashing by.

'This is Ethan,' Travis says to her. 'My brother, Ethan.'

We shake hands and Sarah, the doctor, watches the machine for a while as Sebastian adjusts the drip.

'Why don't you guys take a break and I'll sit with your mum for a bit,' Sarah says and we both look at Joy, who nods that she thinks this is a fine idea.

Sebastian points us in the direction of the cafeteria but I've been here before.

As sugar dissolves into our coffees Travis, looking lost, fills me in.

'The on-call doctor decided this morning to admit her,' Travis tells me. 'The pain was so bad and she needed her lungs drained.'

I say nothing – it's the least I can do.

'Sarah called me this afternoon. She said she'd had a good talk with Mum and they'd decided to increase her medication.' Travis looks at me. 'Sharply.'

I put my hand on his shoulder. And continue to say nothing.

'Is this happening?' Travis asks me.

'I think it is, Trav,' I say.

He cries now.

Sarah finds us with our full cups of cold coffee. She takes a seat, and a moment, before suggesting we go in one at a time. Joy wants to see us.

I leave Travis with Sarah and walk the corridor on loose legs. As I ease the door open Joy moves her eyes and tracks me without blinking as I sit down beside her, taking her hand.

'Ethan,' her voice is soft but no less Joy than I've known.

'Yes?'

'Can you look in my handbag for me?'

I pull her handbag over from the table and open it.

'There should be a piece of paper,' she tells me. 'Folded up.'

'Got it,' I say, unfolding the paper.

It's the page from my old schoolbook, the one where I'd listed what I wanted for my future. There's a fresh tick against the word 'Forza'.

'I'm going to have to relinquish my place in the gang, Ethan.'

'I love you,' I say and Joy closes her eyes for a beat.

'You know what I wished for?' Joy asks me.

'Travis,' I say. 'Oh, and to see Japan.'

Joy laughs. I swear it was a laugh!

'And I did too,' she says, adding, 'but after having Travis, what I've wanted most was to give him a family.'

I smile at her and hold her hand even tighter – she seems more than able to bear it.

'Your dad wanted to leave you a family as well,' she tells me.

'So I guess Travis gets the house!' I say, feigning jealousy, and we both laugh now – without releasing hands for even a moment.

'Aah, but you, Ethan,' Joy says. 'You, I'm leaving Travis.'

'How much do you reckon Cash Convertors will give me for him?'

She likes that.

'I should fetch Travis now,' I say.

Without a further word I kiss Joy gently on the forehead and leave her side.

33. Joyless

Again I'm awake with the old folk, waiting for the world to start. The best part of each of the past few days has been those first moments before my operating system has had a chance to fully load. And now, like Windows Vista, it's entirely crap.

F-day. Friday. Funeral day. Fucked day. The end of this week stings worse than any Monday morning. Celeste insisted I turn up the last few days – apparently *step* is not real enough for her. Ironically she did me a favour – their lunacy was a relief. Tomorrow the advert runs *and* I'm expected to commence my stakeout at the Clarion. I shouldn't imagine they'll want any more from me after that.

Having roamed down Swanston, with its random dried eruptions of Thursday night puke, before continuing far enough out to where the dog people collect turds in plastic bags, it all feels like excrement. Now I walk back into full daylight and into that fucking suit.

■ ■ ■

We three sit in Baxter's. Bizarrely, it's the first time I've ever had a drink here.

'Your mum's friends are really nice,' Alejandra tells Travis.

Travis loosens his tie and I follow suit.

'They are,' Travis agrees.

Joy's farewell wasn't the strictly solemn event I'd feared. There *were* the vases of freshly executed roses and the coldness of the brass-adorned coffin, but there was also her favourite music, some great reminiscences from her mates, and an unfaltering Travis who never once looked like he'd drop her.

Travis insists on buying the next jug and I look at Alejandra. This is the first time we've been alone in weeks. She glances down at her red silk blouse.

'Joy told me I was not to wear black to her funeral.'

'Did she?'

'I hope people didn't think it was poor form on my part.'

I'm about to remind her she never seems to care what people think of her and then I remember the whole weight thing. It's a perfect time to tell her about the happenings at Tate Lane and to find out what she's been up to since she was marched out. No, it really isn't the perfect time, so I let it all go unexplained for a bit longer.

Travis tops up our glasses without spilling a drop.

'I'm getting better each day,' he notes.

'Have you been eating, Travis?' asks Alejandra, who has cut her own eating back to a needs-only basis.

'Mum's friends have delivered so many still-warm casserole dishes that even Diego has stopped looking inside them.'

'Again you're inundated with middle-aged women bearing gifts,' Alejandra says with the perfect pitch of levity – so it should be okay.

Travis laughs out loud, which makes it even better than okay.

■ ■ ■

'Thirty-seven, please.'

'Thirty-seven?' Zhen asks incredulously.

'Uh-huh,' I say.

Is he so uncertain because he actually does connect me to 52 and I'm not invisible after all, *or* is there something intrinsically wrong with 37?

The bug zapper drops the occasional mosquito corpse onto my coat's lapel and I simply brush them off. I stick to my guns of not looking at the menu board to see what the fuck 37 is other than the first number that came into my brain. The beer that's already washed through that very brain swishes inside my stomach each time I switch my crossed legs over and back again. Travis will be heating up a casserole of neighbourly concern whilst Alejandra will be sitting down with her family, and Damien, all of them scrutinising her plate.

Surely it wouldn't be on the menu if there were something wrong with it.

'Thirty-seven. Ready.'

Zhen hands me my dinner, already plastic-bagged and forked, but I decide to return to my seat and eat in. This place won't know what's hit it. Maybe next time I'll bring a friend and the entire world will have flipped.

I peel off the lid – there is something wrong with it! Looking gives no clue and neither does sniffing. I've no idea what animal or collection of animals this is. They've included a menu in the bag – maybe Zhen is suggesting I need assistance or appreciates I'm mixing it up finally. Or maybe there's always a menu in the bag. My finger rolls down the list, allowing my eyes to focus more easily. *Mixed Spices Intestine.*

Sounds worse than it tastes.

34. Three

From the street it's the same as from my window and I stand entirely still, mesmerised by the progression. For years time has stood still according to the clock atop the town hall. Now it's fairly racing.

Satisfied that it's not an optical illusion, I cross back across the tram lines toward Baxter's and the guy recognises me first.

'Ethan?'

It's Damien, Alejandra's Damien.

'Yeah,' I say as casually as I can, 'Damien.'

'How's Alejandra?' *He* asks *me*.

'I was going to ask you that,' I say, unsure exactly how fast time has raced by since I last checked, and further confused by the realisation the blonde next to Damien is *with* Damien.

She elbows him and he tells me, 'This is Ursula.'

We both say hi.

'I last saw Alejandra nearly three weeks back,' Damien says, while Ursula gazes off into the distance. 'She went for a run on the treadmill and never returned.'

'She's probably about thirty-five kilos by now,' Ursula says, rejoining us momentarily, and they both grin.

Of course I saw Alejandra at Joy's funeral only a week back so I know she's okay. She never mentioned this, however.

'Have you heard from her though?' I ask Damien.

'Once – to tell me she's moved into a post office box, so far as I'm to know.'

Damien doesn't seem to be particularly relieved that I'm as clueless as he is on the topic of Alejandra. He's moved on already, it seems, and Ursula is keen to keep moving, so we say goodbye.

I immediately race upstairs to find my mobile and, without my usual procrastination, send the text. And wait. Nothing is more disappointing than silence, except maybe hearing something hit your inbox then finding it's a promotional message from Telstra.

It rings. The Telstra Corporation never calls me.

'Hey Ethan,' Alejandra says as if all is cool with her.

'Hey,' I say, before diving right in. 'I just ran into Damien – he said you moved out.'

'I would have said something but with me leaving work, and Joy, I just thought I'd wait a bit.'

'Okay,' I say, feeling a little sidelined.

'It needed to be about me and Damien, not you and me. Not us.'

Us?

'Are you staying at your folks?' I ask.

'Yes, the triplets are all back together in the same bedroom,' Alejandra replies, laughing, and then, 'So where are you now?'

Cloud nine as it happens.

'Baxter's,' I say. 'Upstairs. You?'

'Downstairs.'

'Huh?'

'I was round the corner when you texted,' Alejandra says.

'I'm coming down.'

The Saturday crowd is in place and I head towards Alejandra. She's wearing blue jeans and a yellow T-shirt.

'Hey,' we say.

'Beer?' I ask.

'Definitely – we have a lot of catching up,' Alejandra says, smiling, and then calls after me, 'Oh, Ethan – fetch a menu, would you?'

'They do food here?' I mouth.

She laughs.

When I return Alejandra asks me, 'So how is Travis doing?'

'I've spoken to him every day – each call gets a little bit longer, so I think he's getting there.'

'What's he going to do?'

'His agency has been bugging him to go to New York but he reckons there's more than enough superficiality here.'

I'm still deciding whether to interrogate Alejandra about Damien or just let it alone when she pulls out the Tate Lane advert for her job from her handbag, torn from last weekend's paper.

'I loved this!' Alejandra says with a huge smile.

'That asterisk by the company logo cost me my job,' I say with mock gloom.

'At last, honesty in advertising: *may contain nuts,*' Alejandra reads the fine print. 'So what did Celeste say on Monday morning?'

'I knew not to front,' I reply. 'She'd also given me an assignment for the same weekend and I failed to deliver on that as well, so there wasn't much point riding her stinking lift one more time.'

Next to us an old lady dithers about whether she should risk cream with dessert before eventually denying herself.

Alejandra whispers, 'She's at least seventy!'

'What are you having?' I ask.

After deciding on a slab of lemon meringue pie she tells me, 'To think I used to imagine I was five kilos from happy.'

'Maybe you were,' I say. 'Five kilos shy, that is.'

She looks at me.

'Did that sound rude?' I say, blushing. 'You know what I mean.'

'I know,' Alejandra says with a laugh.

Two rare events: I have my mobile with me *and* it rings.

'Hey Trav,' I say.

'Hey – where are you at?'

'Baxter's.'

'Maybe it's time to move out of there, Ethan,' Travis says. 'Want to have a drink at the bar without a name?'

'Sure,' I reply. 'I'll bring Alejandra.'

■ ■ ■

'It'll be the same empty crowd – the only thing they'll have over the fakeness level here is at least *their* American accents will be genuine …'

Travis is talking to Alejandra as I return with a round …

'… and anyway I still have family here.'

… just in time.

'Have you heard from Zac recently?' Alejandra asks Travis.

'Just via Twitter – Tuesday he was "stoked about his hair" and yesterday he was "going to try cranberry juice for the first time".'

'Wow,' Alejandra says.

'I'm no longer a follower,' Travis says.

The afternoon crowd is settling in and Oscar smiles at us as he passes, adding our empty jug to his collection.

Travis puts his beer down suddenly as if preparing to commence a speech.

'Oscar asked me to consider taking this place over from him.'

'How do you mean?' I ask.

'I came in last week and mentioned how Mum thought I'd be good at running a joint like this.'

'She did?'

'Yeah. Since that night we came by she kept telling me to consider it.'

'So is Oscar ready to sell?' Alejandra asks.

'He reckons he'll fit in with me if I'm serious.'

'Are you?' I ask.

'I think so,' Travis says, looking a little daunted already.

'Let me know if you need some help.' I say.

'I need some help,' Travis says immediately.

My normally cautious mind races over the speed humps as if they're nonexistent.

Travis looks at me silently and I say, 'Between us we have two places to sell. I'm in.'

'Two and a half,' Alejandra says.

'Are you serious?' Travis says to both of us.

'Why not?' I say and Travis high-fives me.

'*¿Porqué no?*' Alejandra says.

'Is that good?' Travis asks me.

'Nope,' I say. 'It's fucking awesome.'

In the dead of winter plans seem overwhelming, but here, at the height of spring, it all feels so possible.

Travis is suddenly in flight – we can all live upstairs, he and I can run the bar, and Alejandra – who once declared that people are fine … as an abstract notion – can run the kitchen. With Travis in the front-of-house, Alejandra back-of-house, I'm in *the* house – a house which isn't empty when all the lights have gone out.

'Are we really doing this?' Travis gives me a smile I recognise – Joy's smile.

'Yes, we are,' I reply.

'My round,' Travis says and bounds off to the bar.

'I think we're here for a while,' Alejandra says.

'I've got some fish to buy,' I tell her suddenly. 'Some mates for Mister Fantastic.'

She smiles at me, *that* smile, and it looks set to last.